MURDER IN REPROACH

ANNE CLEELAND

ARTEMIS
PRESS

THE DOYLE & ACTON MYSTERY SERIES IN ORDER:

Murder in Thrall

Murder in Retribution

Murder in Hindsight

Murder in Containment

Murder in All Honour

Murder in Shadow

Murder in Misdirection

Murder in Spite

Murder in Just Cause

Murder in the Blood

Murder in Deep Regret

Murder in Revelation

Murder in Unsound Mind

Murder in Material Gain

Murder in Immunity

Murder in All Fury

Murder in Admonishment

Murder in Protocol

Murder in Reproach

For Stephanie Laurens, who can write a ripping redemption love-story; and for all others like her.

CHAPTER 1

"Not much to see, Munoz," Doyle said doubtfully. "It looks to be a classic reproach-suicide."

The two Scotland Yard detectives were taking a long, assessing look at the decedent, a wealthy woman who'd apparently decided to end her own life. She was perhaps forty years old, and laid-out atop the coverlet on her own bed—dressed in a silk dressing gown complete with matching slippers, the kind with the fancy little fluff balls on the toes. She was well-coifed and wearing make-up, and between the hands that rested on her breast she held a single peacock feather.

"Yes. Definitely staged," Munoz remarked.

As a practical matter, suicides tended to take two different routes; either the person dispatched themselves simply and efficiently because they didn't want to be alive any longer, or they killed themselves as a reproach to another person—usually their significant other. Reproach-suicides were either very bloody—

the decedent wanted to shock—or the reproach instead sought to invoke guilt, which meant that the scene looked rather like the one laid out before them—carefully staged so as to maximize the reproach.

"We're here why?" asked Munoz in an annoyed tone. She and Doyle were both homicide detectives, and suicides were normally covered by a regular field-officer, who would then call-in a Coroner's assistant to confirm a self-inflicted death. No point in spending any of the CID's budget when the cause of death was cut-and-dried.

"The housekeeper," Doyle reminded her. "The field-officer says the housekeeper's the one who found her this morning, and she insists it isn't a suicide. And no need to be so cross; if you have to go throw-up, I'll cover for you."

"I'm *fine*, Doyle," Munoz retorted. She was newly-pregnant, and like a bear with a sore head about it; Munoz was one who was used to being in control, and there was nothing like morning-sickness to bring home the fact that any control you thought you had over your life was going to disappear for the next eighteen years or so.

"Shall I tape the scene?" Doyle ventured. Munoz had been lately promoted to Inspector, and so she was the lead on the case—a fact that would have rankled, back in the day, but which now didn't seem nearly as important to Doyle as it used to. Munoz would no doubt discover this, too; having little children made one step back a bit, and recalculate one's priorities.

"Let's go interview the housekeeper, first," Munoz replied. "Then we can decide whether any further procedure is just going to be a waste of time."

They left the bedroom and made their way down the stairs to the main room. The townhouse was one of those elegant, refurbished places that populated the West End of London—the ones that made no bones about the fact that the owner was very wealthy and not ashamed to let everyone know. Not a lot of homicides, in this area of town, since the people who could afford such places had the means to install high-end security equipment.

The housekeeper's pale face looked up at them from her position on the sofa, watching as they descended the stairs. It was clear that the young woman was genuinely distraught—her hair was in disarray and her eyes reddened from weeping; in her hand, she held a wadded-up handkerchief.

"I'm very sorry for your loss," Munoz began, and then checked her notes. "Miss Senak."

"Why? Why would someone kill her?" the young woman asked in a hushed tone, her lips trembling as she looked at each of them in turn. "Why would they do such a thing?"

"I'll have to ask you some questions about it," Munoz replied. "Would that be all right?"

The witness took a long, shuddering breath and dabbed at her eyes with her handkerchief. "Yes, yes—of course."

She'd an accent, and Doyle guessed that she was Eastern European—Doyle wasn't good at accents, being as everyone who wasn't Irish tended to have a very strange one. And it was interesting that the witness seemed genuinely cut-up about the death—you wouldn't think a young housekeeper—she'd be mid-twenties, Doyle guessed—would be quite so distraught. But Doyle knew that Ms. Senak's distress was indeed genuine and not feigned; Doyle had a highly-developed intuitive sense—was what the Irish would call 'fey'—and this preceptive ability meant that she was very sensitive to other people's emotions. As an added bonus, she could usually tell when someone was lying, which had been very helpful in her career as a detective, because it enabled her to sort-out the wheat from the chaff, so to speak. But it also meant that she had to tread warily; few knew of her abilities, and the last needful thing was to allow the general public to catch-on to the fact that Officer Doyle had strange and unquantifiable powers.

Munoz asked, "How long have you been the housekeeper for Mrs. Waring?"

"Just over one year," the witness whispered.

"Were you hired through an agency?"

"No—I met Mrs. Waring at the theatre. I wished to be an actress in one of her plays—I was trying out for a part."

Munoz nodded as she checked the notes on her tablet—they'd pulled up the decedent's personal information on the way over. "Mrs. Waring was herself an actress when she was younger," Munoz read. "She quit acting to marry Basil Waring—the theatre producer—about four years ago, but then he died shortly after."

Munoz paused to look up, and asked in a casual tone, "Four years is plenty of time to start dating again; was Mrs. Waring seeing anyone?"

This was an important question, since the suicide appeared to be a reproach to someone, but the witness shook her head. "No. She wasn't allowed—not after Sally died."

Both Doyle and Munoz stared at her for a moment, and then Munoz asked, "Wasn't allowed by who?"

In a stricken voice, the witness explained, "The others—the theatre-people, who wanted to use her money. They bullied her—the one man was a terrible bully." Her lips started trembling again, and so she bent her head and brought her handkerchief to her mouth.

Munoz cast Doyle an I-told-you-so glance, in that the bullying theatre-people would make an excellent reason to stage this rather dramatic reproach-suicide. "So; she wasn't happy with her colleagues. And I suppose she missed her husband—Sally, she called him?"

The young woman paused, and then admitted, "I do not know if she missed him. She never spoke of him to me."

Again, Munoz checked her notes. "And you came back from your day off this morning to discover that she was dead."

"Yes," the girl whispered. "Who could have done this?"

Doyle gave Munoz a quick glance, because usually you asked the witness to recite events step-by-step without referring to the field-officer's notes, being as you wanted to see if their story had changed in the meantime. However, it seemed clear that Munoz was in a bit of a hurry, poor thing, and so Doyle decided to cut to the nub and find out what it was they needed to find out. "Why d'you think someone killed Mrs. Waring, Miss Senak? If she was that unhappy, she may have wanted to end her life."

The young woman stared at her in surprise. "Oh, no—no." With growing conviction, she shook her head as she looked at both detectives. "No—she would not have—never; she was not brave enough to do such a thing."

"You never know, and it does sound as though she was unhappy," Doyle suggested gently.

"No—she was not thinking of death," the young woman repeated adamantly. "She was happy about the reception, and asked me what she should wear to it."

"Which reception is this, now?"

"At the theatre, this weekend."

Munoz knit her brow. "I thought she didn't like the theatre-people."

Sadly, the witness shook her head. "She always did what they told her to, because they kept her in this nice house, and made much of her. But she was like a bird in a cage." The young woman drew a long breath, thinking about this. "And they would do something to please her, when they knew that she was unhappy. They were going to hang her portrait in the theatre—this was the reason for the reception. She was very pleased by this—that her portrait would hang in the theatre." Again, she shook her head slowly. "She would not have killed herself—no."

"I'll be right back," Munoz interrupted abruptly, and rose to stride over toward the powder room.

"Mayhap you are mistaken," Doyle told the witness, touching the young woman's knee with a gentle hand. "It doesn't sound as though she was very happy, to me. A lot of rich people aren't."

But the witness only replied with some conviction, "No—she was not strong. I said to her—maybe you must speak with an attorney, yes? But she was not strong. And so, she was not strong enough to kill herself—don't you see? Instead, someone has killed her, but I don't know who would do such a thing."

Doyle decided she may as well ask a few homicide-questions,

even though it seemed more and more clear that this was indeed a suicide. And in any event, she should stall so as to cover for poor Munoz. "Who would want to kill her, d'you think? Did she have a fight with one of these theatre-people?"

"No—no," the witness disclaimed immediately. "The theatre-people would not want to kill her—she was—" here she paused, as though searching for the words. "She was like a—like a puppet, and they needed to use her. Use her name, and her money."

Doyle's scalp prickled, which was what it did when her intuition was prodding her to pay attention, and—rather surprised that she'd been thus prompted—she decided that she may as well ask another homicide-question. "Who gets her money, when she dies?"

The young woman looked at her blankly. "I do not know."

"Not you?" Doyle teased with a smile, even though the question had merit; it was a staple of homicide investigation that you always took a long look at the first-reporter. However, it seemed very unlikely that this young woman was a suspect; she was obviously fond of her former mistress, and in Doyle's view she was no killer—not to mention that it would be a strange sort of killer who would be fighting so hard to pull the case out of a suicide-designation.

"She gave me her pearls," the witness whispered, stricken. "Should I give them back?"

Doyle decided to take the bull by the horns. "Only if you killed her. Did you?"

"Oh—no, no," Miss Senak disclaimed, horrified by the very thought.

"Then you should keep the pearls," Doyle decided. "They were a gift, after all."

At this point, Munoz returned, looking a bit less green-about-the-gills. "Let's confer, Sergeant."

It seemed clear that Munoz wanted to compare notes and finish up, but Doyle was still a bit perplexed about why her intuition had acted up—it was that remark about how the theatre-people wanted to use the dead woman's name and money, which truly shouldn't be much of a news-flash. Not to mention that the remark seemed to undermine the housekeeper's own suspicions; if the theatre-people—who seemed to feature as the villains in this tale—didn't want the decedent dead, then who did?

With a knit brow, Doyle gave it once last attempt. "Aside from her lookin' forward to the reception, and your own sense that Mrs. Waring wouldn't kill herself, can you think of any other reason you believe she might have been murdered?"

"It doesn't look to be a murder," Munoz pointed out a bit brusquely, since she was the lead, after all, and the clock was ticking before her next visit to the loo. "It seems unlikely that Mrs. Waring's body would have been staged the way it was, if that was the case."

As though reminded, the witness lifted her face to exclaim, "Yes—yes, it was staged—there was the feather." With an air of triumph, she declared, "*This* is how I know."

Munoz frowned slightly. "What about the feather?"

In all sincerity, the witness explained, "Mrs. Waring would never have brought a peacock feather into the house—peacock feathers are bad luck."

CHAPTER 2

"Doyle's worried there might be something here," Munoz was explaining to Detective Inspector Thomas Williams, as he stood with the two women in a corner of the drawing room. Williams been called-in for a consult, since he would be assigned as the Senior Investigating Officer if a file were indeed to be opened. It was a familiar role for the young man, ever since Doyle had married Chief Inspector Acton. Doyle's husband—who could control her assignments—liked to have Williams handle her cases because he knew that Williams would keep a watchful eye on her. Not that she had many cases to begin with; Doyle's caseload was fairly light because she worked part-time, due to having two small boys at home.

Despite his friendship with Doyle, however, Williams was a busy man and not about to open a case-file where it wasn't warranted, and so he immediately began firing-off questions. "No one else lived here?"

"No—just Mrs. Waring and the housekeeper." Munoz bent her head to check the field-officer's notes. "They would have the occasional fundraiser here, but nothing of that sort lately."

"Who has a key?"

"It's a code, and it's unclear how many have it."

"Who gets her money?"

"Again, not clear as yet."

"What do her electronics show?"

"The housekeeper said she didn't have a mobile—only a land-line."

Williams paused in surprise. "Really?"

"Hard to believe," Doyle agreed. "She wasn't very old, but mayhap she was old-fashioned. Apparently, she didn't do much, outside the theatre—didn't leave the house much. The housekeeper seems to think she was a bit brow-beaten by the theatre-people."

Williams cocked his head. "Lonely and bullied. A good reason to kill yourself."

"Aye," Doyle agreed fairly. "But the housekeeper is certain that's not the case, and she seems to think the peacock feather is the proof."

Skeptical, Williams remarked, "I don't know about that; the decedent may have brought-in the peacock feather because she was going to kill herself—she wanted to be dramatic about it."

Almost reluctantly, Munoz pointed out, "But if that were the case, she must have wanted it to be seen, and seen by someone who'd know what it meant—otherwise she'd just kill herself with no fuss. If this was a reproach-suicide, who was being reproached? It doesn't seem to be the housekeeper."

"Definitely not," said Doyle, with a quick glance at Williams. He was the only person—aside from Acton, her husband—who knew of her ability to sense the truth, and she wanted him to know that the housekeeper wasn't the killer—if there was indeed a killer in the first place, of course.

Williams thought this over. "Has next-of-kin been notified?"

"We don't have one, as yet," Munoz replied. "She was a widow without children, and we've no phone to look into. The housekeeper says she doesn't know of any relatives."

They were interrupted by a field-officer, who'd come to the drawing room doorway to announce a visitor. "A Mr. Grainston, who says he is from the Majestic Theatre. He's very insistent."

"A theatre-person," Doyle observed. "Right on cue."

"Let him in," Munoz directed.

A very sleek-looking older man was escorted within, and he immediately glanced around the room and then looked up the stairway with a worried expression. "What has happened? Is Tricia all right? I saw the police outside."

"I'm afraid Mrs. Waring has passed away," Munoz informed him. "I'm so sorry." Behind their sympathetic expressions, all three detectives were watching the man's reaction very carefully.

He stared at them, his mouth falling open. "*No*," he breathed. "Oh my God—how?"

"I'm very sorry for your loss," said Munoz as she took his arm and steered him toward the sofa. "Come, sit down. Are you related to Mrs. Waring?"

The man seemed to be having some trouble pulling his wits together, and again, his gaze traveled up the stairway. "No—no, I am Jeremy Grainston; I produce plays." He looked at them again, rather blankly. "What happened? Did she fall?"

But Munoz was the one asking questions, here. "Could you direct us to her next of kin, Mr. Grainston? It would be very helpful."

Slowly, he replied, "I think she had family in the Midlands—but I don't think she's seen them in a long while. She was married to Sally, of course, but he died a few years back." He paused, and then abruptly bent his head to rest it in his hands. "Oh my God—I can't believe this."

"Did you have an appointment with her, this morning?" Williams asked in a mild tone, and Doyle knew Williams was thinking that mayhap this fellow was the object of Mrs. Waring's reproach.

"No—no, but I was driving by—it's on my route to the theatre. Sometimes I drop in, to say hallo."

"Every morning, or just occasionally?" Williams asked, still testing-out his theory.

"Maybe once a week." This was the truth, and Doyle met Williams' eyes in affirmation.

"You were friends?" Munoz asked, with a show of sympathy.

He let out a breath. "I suppose you could say that. Tricia was something of an icon, in theatre circles. Or, more correctly, Sally was—her late husband. He'd been instrumental in keeping the district going, and raising funds through some tough times. Tricia took over for him after he died." He paused, and again said slowly, "I can't believe she's dead." He lifted his face to Williams. "How did she die?"

Munoz answered, "That's not clear, as yet."

"May I see her?"

"No—I'm afraid that's only for next-of-kin."

There was a small silence, and—probing, a bit—Doyle remarked, "I understand Mrs. Waring was goin' to a reception, this comin' weekend."

He nodded. "Yes. We were going to unveil her portrait at a fundraiser."

"Bad luck," Williams offered.

Reminded, the man asked, "Do you suppose I could take her portrait to the theatre? It's here, somewhere—I was dropping by this morning to see if I could pick it up. The theatre's foundation commissioned it, and I can show that we paid for it. We can still hang it, in honor of her life."

"Nothing in or out of the house at the present time," Munoz informed him. After a slight pause, she added, "We have to rule out homicide."

Blinking in surprise, the man quickly assured them, "Oh—no one would want to kill her—she wouldn't hurt a fly."

Again, Doyle met Williams' eyes because—surprisingly—this was the truth.

CHAPTER 3

Munoz had retreated to the loo again, and so Doyle and Williams were taking the opportunity to confer, with Williams stating, "So; Grainston didn't kill her."

"No," Doyle affirmed. "Neither did the housekeeper."

Lifting a shoulder, Williams remarked, "I don't know as we've any other suspects, Kath. No visitors, no sign of a break-in, and no trauma to the body."

Doyle knit her brow. "I know, but its pingin' my radar, Thomas. The housekeeper seems certain that there was foul play, and I have to say that I'm inclined to believe her, even though I know it doesn't make much sense."

He drew a resigned breath. "Right, then. I'll open a preliminary file, and we'll see what we can find out, starting with who gets her money."

But Doyle pointed out, "I'm not sure about the inheritanceangle, Thomas; if someone's killed her for her money, why would they take the trouble of stagin' her suicide as a reproach? The killer would just spike her drink, put her to bed, and call it a day."

"Right—that's a good point; the killer wouldn't want to raise any questions. Which swings it back to a reproach-suicide, since there's no such thing as a reproach-murder."

"I suppose not," Doyle agreed.

He cast her a glance. "What did you think of the theatre-fellow? Any chance he was having an affair with her, and threw her over? Maybe that's who she wanted to reproach."

Frowning, Doyle shook her head slightly. "I don't have that sense—not a shred of guilt to be found, and the housekeeper said the decedent wasn't seein' anyone; she'd surely know if these two were havin' an affair. Although I will say that Grainston's truly shook; I don't know if he's shook because he was fond of her, or if he's shook because her death is a problem for him."

Thoughtfully, Williams offered, "Why would it be a problem, though? If there are no children or relatives in the picture, we can presume she'll leave her fortune to the theatre, right? You'd think he'd be happy he didn't have to cater to her anymore."

But Doyle explained, "Apparently, they liked to trot her out to help raise money, bein' as she was married to the great man. I think that was her main role, according to the housekeeper, so it does sound as though her death is something of a blow to the theatre."

He lifted a brow. "Maybe she wasn't happy, being a fund-raising prop."

Doyle admitted, "Aye, the housekeeper indicated as much. She said the decedent was like a bird in a cage."

"Suicide," he pronounced.

"It does make a good case," she reluctantly agreed.

He blew out a breath. "All right. If there's any chance this is a homicide, it must be about the money, so let's find out who gets it as a priority. If it goes where everyone expected it to, I'm going to swing even harder toward suicide."

Doyle made a note in her tablet. "Will do." Reminded, she looked up at him. "How's it goin' on your own money-case?"

He grimaced. "It's a rabbit hole, naturally. We're having fits trying to put together hard evidence—we haven't managed to get a search-warrant on the little that we have."

Doyle made a sound of sympathy. "I can't say I'm surprised; it would be a major take-down, and the warrant-magistrates are nervous-nellies, sometimes."

Recently, they'd come across what looked to be a money-laundering conspiracy that involved the international sale of fake artwork—something they'd run across several times before. Rare coins and artwork were often sold at inflated prices as a means to launder money outside of the banking system, and—since there weren't enough of either to cover the illicit demand—oftentimes the coins and artwork were faked. And there was an added bonus for the villains in a fake-artwork scheme, in that the purchasers could credibly disclaim any ill-intent other than the fact they'd paid too much for a piece of art that turned out to be fake. It was therefore not easy for the CID to build a credible criminal case, which was exactly why these types of schemes tended to persist.

Doyle was determined to keep close tabs on this particular

case, though, mainly because her husband, Chief Inspector Acton, was the overseeing officer and whenever there was untraceable money washing about, he tended to be sorely tempted to dip his fingers into it. A sad state of affairs, but there it was and she'd best look lively.

Doyle had first met her husband when she'd been paired-up with him as a rookie detective—much to everyone's surprise, since Acton tended to avoid junior officers as an unnecessary annoyance. Famously brusque and reclusive, these traits were forgiven him because he'd gained a sterling reputation as the solver of thorny crimes. The public loved him, partly because he was an aristocrat—and they loved it whenever an aristocrat did anything remotely useful—and partly because he was the next thing to a hermit, and therefore intriguingly mysterious.

As a consequence, that selfsame public was astonished when he up and married his rookie partner with no warning whatsoever. To be fair, Doyle was equally astonished, having herself received no warning whatsoever.

She'd soon discovered why Acton had wanted to avoid any sort of courtship; he wanted her to be bound by the bonds of wedlock before she found out that he was not at all what he seemed to his admiring public. Instead, he was something of a vigilante, and his stellar record at the CID had much to do with the fact that he was not above manipulating the evidence so as to send the appropriate villains off to prison. And—even worse—Acton had no problem dispatching those self-same villains himself, if he was concerned that a savvy attorney might convince a jury to let them go; Acton didn't shy away from the occasional murder, whenever he deemed it necessary.

As a newly-minted detective, Doyle had been horrified by these discoveries and she'd immediately starting working to change her husband's murky ways—after all, he truly loved her, and so she was perhaps the only person in the world who could hope to be of some influence. And in this, she'd been somewhat correct; over the course of their marriage there'd been much progress made—a few setbacks, here and there—but overall, she felt she'd helped to put the man's feet on a better path—thank God fastin'. And they'd two young sons now, which helped considerably; having small children underfoot truly cut into one's masterminding-time.

Nonetheless, she'd long-ago realized that there was nothing Acton enjoyed more than diverting large sums of illicit money into the House of Acton's coffers—as long as no one would be the wiser—and this was why she was keeping careful watch on this fake-artwork case. It was akin to putting the fox in charge of the henhouse—there was nothing like some juicy, unidentifiable assets to tempt her husband into committing a few felonies, himself.

William's voice broke into her thoughts. "How's Munoz handling things?"

Doyle smiled. "Just as you'd expect."

They both chuckled in the manner of veteran parents.

She asked, "How're you and yours?"

"Everyone's great. Getting adjusted, of course." Williams and his wife had just welcomed a second son into their family. "I'd give my eyeteeth for a good night's sleep."

"I don't think anyone ever gets adjusted, Thomas—you just

learn to make do with less sleep and more coffee. And speakin' of such, we're havin' another."

He grinned at her. "Are you? Congratulations, Kath."

"I'm keepin' it under my hat, for now, in deference to our Munoz. I'm not feelin' sick—or not yet, leastways—and she'd probably shoot me dead out of spite."

"Got it."

Munoz returned, and both Doyle and Williams knew better than to ask how the Spanish woman was feeling. Instead, Williams informed her, "We think it may be worthwhile to open a preliminary file, mainly to see who gets the decedent's money. Although Doyle pointed out that there would be no point in staging the suicide so elaborately, if the motive was money."

"The whole thing's weird," Munoz pronounced a bit crossly, mainly because she was sick of being sick. "It seems like a classic reproach-suicide, but the housekeeper would surely know if the decedent was having a love-affair."

"Agreed," said Doyle.

Munoz continued, "I suppose since we're looking into motive, we may as well take a quick look at opportunity, too—although if there was an access code for the house, the decedent could have given it out to anyone. Let's take a look at the street-view CCTV for the past couple of days—see if we can get film of who went in and out." She glanced up at the corners of the ceiling. "I didn't see any monitoring equipment on the premises."

"That's a bit odd, in itself," Doyle offered, as she made notes. "Havin' this fancy place, and all."

"She didn't have a mobile, either," Williams reminded them. "She may have been tech-averse."

"True. I suppose if we're going to open a prelim, we should go up and have another look at the scene," Munoz suggested, and the three detectives mounted the stairs again to make a more thorough evaluation.

They paused in the doorway of the bedroom suite to take a long look at the still figure of the dead woman, well-dressed and lying in the elegantly-appointed bed, holding her peacock feather.

"Shall I call-in forensics?" Munoz asked Williams. This was a good question, since a SOCO team would be expensive.

"I vote no," he replied. "We've no bodily fluids to speak of, and we're not going to have much luck trying to get touch-DNA off her clothing or the bed linen."

"Or the feather," Doyle added.

"Or the feather," he agreed.

"Here's a question; if we're assumin' she took pills, how did she take them?" Doyle asked. "There's no glass on the bedside table."

Munoz replied, "The report says there's a water glass in the loo, but it looks clean. No visible prints."

Doyle frowned, thinking about this. "So, she took her pills and then washed her prints off the glass before lyin' down? That seems a bit strange."

"On the other hand, if she was staging a suicide, she may have wanted everything in place," Williams pointed out. "Everything looks tidy in here, and she's well-dressed."

"I suppose that's true."

The luxurious suite had an adjacent sitting area, with two overstuffed armchairs positioned next to a large bow window and several books piled atop the table between. The three detectives moved into the area to take a quick look around, but there was nothing to raise any suspicion. The curtains were drawn, and Williams stepped over so as to open them—it was routine to check to see whether there was a neighbor with a line-of-sight into a potential crime scene. Sunlight flooded into the room as they looked out over the small courtyard at the back of the house, and duly noted that the trees screened the windows from any neighbor-views.

"That must be the decedent's portrait," Williams noted, indicating an easel that was standing in the corner of the room.

"This would be a good room for the sitting, with all the natural light," Munoz explained, being as she was something of an artist, herself.

The three walked over to review the portrait that was displayed on the easel. A very life-like Mrs. Waring was seated at an angle and gazing into the distance, in the usual portrait-pose. The woman looked very much the wealthy-benefactress type, handsome but not beautiful, and with an aura of sadness about her as would befit a famous widow.

As she gazed upon the image, Doyle suddenly stilled, her scalp prickling. Oh, she thought in surprise; oh—now, here's a wrinkle. Faith, I've got to tell Acton, and as soon as I can.

"It's a Javid," Munoz noted in admiration, tilting her head as she reviewed the portrait with an expert eye. "You can always tell—she does such amazing work."

The artist was familiar to Doyle, because the famous Persian woman had also painted her own portrait—hers and Acton's. Indeed, their lives had crossed Javid's several times in the past, and not in necessarily pleasant ways. The artist's first husband was an evil man who'd met a bad end at Acton's hands—a memory that still made Doyle mentally flinch. And—come to think of it—that case had arisen from a fake-artwork scheme, too; at the time, Javid was being forced by her awful husband to paint fakes so as to front the scheme.

"Should we release it to the theatre?" Williams asked Munoz. "Or hold it as evidence?"

Shrugging a shoulder, Munoz replied, "I suppose there's no harm in allowing the theatre to take custody, as long as they can show they paid for it. And Grainston did say they'd want to display it at her memorial. If you would just take some video, please."

"Right," said Doyle, pulling out her tablet once again. She took a video of the portrait and its location in the room, and then she quickly took the opportunity to text Acton: "Need to meet. 1." Code One indicated it was not an urgent situation, and after thinking it over, she added "Bench." On occasion, they'd meet at a park bench down the street from headquarters when they needed to speak in privacy, being as privacy was hard to come by —even in his office—when you were a famous Chief Inspector with a busy caseload. And Acton was definitely busy, just now, since he was the supervising officer on Williams' fake-artwork case.

Her husband's answer, as always, came with gratifying promptness. "Text when you are there, it will give me an excuse to leave."

So; he must be in a task-force meeting, which was not something someone like Acton enjoyed very much—unless he was using the opportunity to devise ways to circumvent law enforcement and run his own little operation, something he'd done in the past. Hopefully, those days were now behind him, fingers crossed.

"I'll take the painting downstairs," Williams offered. "We can tell Grainston he can pick it up at the front door."

"Make sure it's dry, first," Munoz warned. "It takes a long time for oil paintings to dry—sometimes weeks. Let me check."

Carefully, Munoz examined the surface with a penlight, and then lightly touched it in several areas. "It's dry. All right; take it downstairs." To Doyle, she said, "Let's get the Coroner in, and request an autopsy. Ask him if I could have a preliminary report by tomorrow, with a tox follow-up, please."

"Yes, ma'am," Doyle said, but found that she was having trouble dragging her gaze away from the portrait of the dead woman, as Williams carefully maneuvered it out the door.

CHAPTER 4

Munoz dropped Doyle at the park's gate on her way back to headquarters, and Doyle promptly texted Acton and then headed toward the secluded bench where they would meet if it was felt that a discussion warranted extra privacy.

Doyle sat down where she could watch the entry-gate, and then rummaged in her rucksack for a tin-wrapped packet. Her pregnancy was starting to make her feel a bit uneven in the mornings, and she'd found that a few bites of a fruit pie—the prepackaged kind that they sold at petrol stations—seemed to help her feel better. Keeping an eye out for her husband, she took a few stealthy bites; Acton was the healthy-eating type, and so he was of the opinion that prepackaged fruit pies were the work of the devil. Which—to be fair—they may well be; they were so very tempting, with their bright sugary syrup, and their crusty, lard-laden shells.

When she spotted his tall figure approaching on the other side of the hedge, she quickly re-wrapped the pastry and had tucked it safely away again by the time he came through the park's wrought-iron gate. A passing mother pushing a pram gave him a second look, after he'd passed her by; Acton was tall and darkly-handsome, and the benign appreciation of a handsome man was something that was hard-wired into the female consciousness, no matter one's circumstances or age. Indeed, it was half the reason Doyle had been willing to marry the man at the drop of a hat—he was not easy to resist.

She smiled and waved in the manner of someone who wouldn't dream of eating anything remotely unhealthy, and lifted her face for his kiss before he sat down beside her. "Thanks for comin', Michael—I know you're busy."

He opened the parcel he'd been carrying. "I am never too busy for you. Here, I brought a salad."

With some misgiving, Doyle watched him pull-out the carryout container. "Please tell me it's not kale."

"It is not kale," he replied, as he pried off the lid. "Mainly berries, with some greens."

"I'm sick *to death* of berries and greens," she groused.

"Just have a few, then," he coaxed. "I will share with you."

With poor grace, she took up a blackberry. "I won't keep you, Michael, but I wanted to let you know that I think Javid may be a witness in the theatre-lady case, and so I thought I'd best check-in with you about how to handle it."

Patiently, her husband ate his own berry and asked, "Tell me about the theatre-lady case, if you would."

"Oh—right, I'm gettin' ahead of myself. I went with Munoz

to take a look at a supposed suicide, because the woman's housekeeper was certain that she'd been murdered, instead."

"This was the call from the West End?"

He'd know where she'd been that morning, because no matter what he was doing or how busy he was, Acton tended to keep track of her whereabouts—she was always his priority, which was something of a mixed blessing, truth to tell, because he'd demonstrated on more than one occasion that he was willing to take some very questionable actions to smooth her way, if he thought it necessary.

"Aye," she replied, as she tentatively nibbled on the blackberry. "The decedent was Tricia Waring, a big supporter of the theatre—rich lady, it looked."

Acton nodded. "Her late husband was Basil Waring, who devoted a great deal of his fortune to funding theatre projects."

With a smile, she paused. "Look at you, knowin' everythin'; doesn't your head get heavy from carryin' all this information about?"

He smiled slightly, but explained, "Basil Waring was always on the CID's radar because he had some questionable known-associates."

Doyle paused in surprise. "Now, isn't that a wrinkle? Like who?"

"Basil Waring's real name was Vasily Warrski, and he tended to fraternize with members of the Russian-mafia."

This was of interest, because one of the underworld factions that the CID did battle with on a regular basis consisted of an assortment of unsavory characters who could loosely be characterized as “Russian-mafia” for want of a better term. And the reason it was an ongoing battle was because this particular brand of villain tended to be clothed as respectable businessmen, courtesy of the pervasive corruption back in their home country. Usually, the bad-actors were bankers laundering money or running a protection-racket and because there was a fine line between robust free enterprise and sharp dealings, the police were often unable to build a credible case against them.

Not to mention the mafia-people were very careful to stay under-the-radar as much as possible. Indeed, if they determined that one of their members was a liability—drawing too much police attention—they would take care of the problem themselves; preemption-murders, the CID called them, and had little sympathy for the victims.

Acton continued, “It wasn’t something that was well-known; Waring had anglicized his name and he kept the connection fairly quiet.”

“Did he have a record?”

“No—although in that community, such a thing doesn’t mean much.”

This was true, in that the oligarchs who funded these questionable enterprises also funded high-quality legal representation—attorneys who were well-skilled in keeping their clients out of trouble.

Thinking about this, Doyle mused, “Everyone called him ‘Sally’—mayhap that’s short for Vasily—although it fits with Basil, too. I don’t think his wife was Russian, though; her bio said she was from the Midlands, if the bio can be believed.”

"Correct; I believe she was a minor stage-actress that he married fairly late in life. She had no known connection to any underworld activities."

Teasing, she offered, "Fancy that; he fell for an underling, same as you."

He smiled at her teasing, even as he tilted his head in mild disagreement. "Basil Waring was generally believed to be interested in men. It was something of a surprise, at the time, when he married his wife."

"Oh. Well, there's another wrinkle." She knit her brow, and chose the smallest raspberry in the bowl. "The housekeeper said Mrs. Waring never spoke of him—which seems strange. Mayhap she was unhappy in her marriage."

"Tell me of your interest in Javid," he prompted gently, being as he was on a strict schedule and the wife of his bosom was taking her sweet time in getting to the point.

"Oh—yes. Well, it looked to be a typical reproach-suicide—carefully staged, with Mrs. Waring dressed to the nines and everythin' neat as a pin."

"She was where?"

"Lyin' on her bed. And holdin' a peacock feather, of all things—all very dramatic and actress-y. The only thing is, it's not clear who was bein' reproached; the housekeeper said she wasn't datin' anyone—said she kept to herself, mostly. No relatives in the area, either."

"The same housekeeper who thinks she was killed?"

"Aye. She's young, and mighty cut-up about it—which seemed a bit odd. Insists her mistress would never have killed herself." Remembering, Doyle added, "The housekeeper seemed to think that the theatre-people were bullying her, a bit—said Mrs. Waring was a bird in a cage, and they were just usin' her for her famous name."

Acton lifted a gooseberry to feed to her, since she'd paused in her healthy-eating endeavors. "Who inherits?"

"I'm tasked with findin' that out today—we're assumin' it's the theatre, since it was Basil Waring's fortune to begin with."

"Yes, I imagine. Let me know if there's a surprise."

She nodded. "And speakin' of such, there was a Jeremy Grainston from the theatre who came by when he saw the coppers hangin' about, and he was truly knocked off his pins to discover she was dead—genuinely upset. They were goin' to hold a fundraiser this weekend, and hang Mrs. Waring's portrait in pride of place at the theatre. The housekeeper seemed to think they were doin' it to jolly her along—what with all the bullyin', and such."

He considered this thoughtfully. "Could the housekeeper be attempting a misdirection play?"

Doyle shook her head. "No, she's not the killer. Instead, she's true-blue, and mighty upset by it all. And it does seem that Mrs. Waring was fond of her—she'd readily confessed that she'd been gifted some jewelry, and it was true. Not to mention that she had to practically beg us to do an investigation in the first place; it truly looked to be a reproach-suicide, save that there's no obvious candidate for the reproachin'."

"Javid painted the portrait," Acton concluded on his own, because his wife tended to give a scattered report, and wander away from the main point.

"Aye—that's why I called you. It was in the decedent's

bedroom, and it gave me a fine case of the willies, Michael." She paused, her brow knit. "I don't think Javid liked Mrs. Waring very much."

CHAPTER 5

This disclosure caught his interest, and he regarded her thoughtfully. Acton tended to be very respectful of his wife's perceptive abilities, being as they'd helped solve many a thorny case—not to mention save the House of Acton on several memorable occasions. "Anything obvious, or just a feeling?"

"Just one of my feelin's, Michael. There was a—a *coldness*, I guess you'd say. It didn't seem in keepin', somehow." Struggling to explain the inexplicable, she offered, "The painting was—it was well-done, at least accordin' to Munoz, but I caught the sense Javid didn't approve of Mrs. Waring. And so—if we assume that the woman was indeed murdered—Javid may know somethin', since the final sittin' was the day before her death. She was one of the last people to see the decedent alive."

"The portrait is completed?"

"Aye; Munoz checked to make sure it was dry, and then she released it to the theatre—they want to hang it at the memorial."

Her husband offered her a strawberry, and with palpable reluctance, Doyle accepted it and continued, "It may be that Mrs. Waring confessed somethin' to Javid durin' her sittin' so as to raise a red flag about who'd want to kill her—somethin' unsavory, that also made Javid unhappy with her. Javid gets a good bead on people durin' these sittings, after all—recall that we think she was the one who raised the alarm about Sasha Lanska; this situation may be somethin' similar."

He nodded thoughtfully, since this was a good point. Sasha Lanska had been a famous theatre actress with a long and illustrious career, but the woman had been brutally murdered—burnt to death—because she'd been involved in a nasty plot to murder a child.

Lanska had been painted by Javid just before she was murdered, and Doyle had guessed that the artist had gleaned some information at the sitting that she'd passed along to her current husband—a famous criminal lawyer named Sir Vikili. Sir Vikili had then, presumably, passed along the tip—under the radar, of course, because famous criminal lawyers had to avoid any hint that they might be willing to grass-out their clients—and the child's murder-plot had been thwarted, with Lanska paying a terrible price for her sins.

Doyle concluded, "So, I think we should interview Javid, to see if she can cast any light on whether this might indeed be a homicide. I think she knows somethin' dicey about Mrs. Waring, Michael—I'm almost sure of it."

Acton offered, "Sasha Lanska was one of Basil Waring's known-associates. He produced many of her plays."

Doyle stared at him. "Another wrinkle. Faith, there's a lot of dots, gettin' themselves connected. And they're both Russian—although he tried to hide that fact, it seems."

"Yes—although it was perhaps in his best interests to do so. Basil Waring—or Warrski, as he was—came from a White Russian heritage."

As she accepted another blackberry, Doyle said, "Remind me what that means, Michael."

"When the Tsar was overthrown, the monarchists who supported him were forced to flee from the Bolsheviks. They were known as White Russians."

Doyle raised her brows. "Oh; we ran into that faction before—when we were dealin' with the Russian Colonel."

"Yes."

She blew out a breath. "Small wonder Basil kept it quiet, then, if he's workin' cheek-by-jowl with the likes of Sasha Lanska; she was a radical through and through—'tis tribes within tribes."

"Indeed."

He said it absently, and Doyle could see that her husband was distracted, thinking, and so she was silent for a few moments, respecting the process and taking the opportunity to surreptitiously ditch the blackberry behind the bench.

"Has Munoz made a decision about how to classify?" he finally asked.

"Williams was called-in for a consult, and they decided to open a preliminary file. I'm to find out who inherits, and who had the entry-code, and take a look at the city CCTV since there weren't any security cameras in the house."

He raised his brows. "That," he said, "is of interest."

"Aye," she agreed. "Although the decedent didn't even have a mobile, so mayhap she was one who didn't like electronics."

"Did you notice any artwork, on the walls?"

Now it was Doyle's turn to raise her brows. "Nothin' that caught my attention, but I wasn't really lookin'. Faith, d'you think this Waring case is somehow connected to your fake-artwork case?"

"It is a possibility. We believe that Denisovich is one of the principals in the rig."

Slowly, Doyle nodded. "Another Russian-mafia type, and just the sort of fellow who'd be hip-deep in such a thing."

They'd run into Igor Denisovich once before, when they'd taken down a money-laundering scheme that was skimming tax-money from public accounts. Denisovich had wriggled off the hook, mainly because the kingpins tended to be very good at insulating themselves—not to mention the infamous Sir Vikili was on a permanent retainer for the aforesaid kingpins.

Doyle offered, "Mayhap that's why Mrs. Waring was murdered—she'd jeopardized the artwork-scheme somehow, and so hers was a preemption-murder."

But he tilted his head in mild disagreement. "Unlikely, since the manner of her death has only invited scrutiny."

"Oh—good point; instead, these villains would just dump her in the channel with none the wiser, in accordance with their usual protocol." She paused, much struck. "Faith, it's a small world, Michael; Javid herself was slated to be a preemption-murder, last time around." This, because when the CID had rolled-up the previous version of the fake-artwork scheme, the artist was going to be tossed into the channel before she could grass-out the other villains. Thoughtfully, Doyle added, "Mayhap that's why she was unhappy with Mrs. Waring—she'd bad memories."

Acton began packing-up their lunch utensils. "I will handle the Javid aspect, but allow me decide how to approach it."

She nodded, since this would be a tangle-patch and was the whole reason she'd met with him for this private discussion. The artist's husband, Sir Vikili, wouldn't be best pleased to have his celebrated wife—who was herself pregnant—questioned as a potential witness in a case against his own clients.

As a matter of form, Acton asked a few follow-up questions. "Had the decedent quarreled with anyone?"

"Not according to the housekeeper—she seemed to think the decedent was browbeaten, and rather timid. And Grainston—the theatre fellow—said that Mrs. Waring wouldn't hurt a fly."

"No forensics to speak of?"

She shook her head. "Williams thought it wouldn't be worth callin' in a team. No prints on the drinkin' glass—didn't even have one at the bedside—and not much to be gained by tryin' to test the bedclothes, or the peacock feather." Reminded, she explained, "The housekeeper seemed to think that was important, Michael—that the decedent was holdin' a peacock feather when she died. She'd been an actress, too, and she said Mrs. Waring would never have brought a peacock feather into the house because they're bad luck."

But Acton didn't seem convinced. "If this was a reproach-suicide, that may have been the entire point."

"Aye; that's what Williams said. But the housekeeper seemed certain." With a little frown, Doyle added, "Seems a strange sort of superstition—that they'd be bad luck; peacock feathers are so very beautiful."

"Yes. More often they symbolize royalty—India's peacock throne is an example."

Teasing, she replied, "Is that so? Then I'm that surprised you don't have a few peacocks wanderin' about at Trestles." Trestles was Acton's hereditary estate, located just a few hours north of London.

With a slight grimace, he explained, "They have the most annoying call—loud and screeching. It is almost unworldly."

"Now, there's a surprise—with them lookin' so mild and elegant."

He checked his watch. "I must go, I'm afraid. Are you headed home or back to headquarters?"

Because she was working part-time, Doyle tended to do field-work every other morning, and then do follow-up work at home whilst their sons were napping. "Home, please—it's easier to concentrate. I've got to shake my stumps and get some answers on this—Munoz wants a preliminary report by tomorrow mornin'."

"If you would, please don't mention Javid's potential as a witness yet."

"Right. Although Munoz may have figured that out for herself—she's a clever beast."

He rose, and offered his hand to help her up. "I would also ask that you find out if the house ever had security cameras, and if it did, when they were removed."

She nodded, since it seemed apparent that he was interested in the possible artwork-scheme connection. “Right.”

“And because you ate some of your salad, I will not object if you finish your fruit pie in the car.”

She laughed at being thus caught out. “Wretched man; how’d you know?”

“I could taste it when I kissed you.”

“Fah—I’d never make a decent criminal, leaving such obvious clues.”

“All part of your charm,” he replied, and fondly threw an arm around her as they headed toward the gate.

CHAPTER 6

That afternoon, Doyle was seated at the kitchen table, working on her report. Acton had an office in their flat's lower level, but Doyle preferred to work at the kitchen table mainly because she could more easily check-in with Reynolds, their butler, about her use of words—she tended to use the wrong words, sometimes, and the spell-check wasn't very helpful if you had it by the wrong leg to begin with. She suspected that Reynolds was well-aware of this, which was why he always seemed to be doing busy-work in the kitchen whenever she was working.

Frowning, she bent to review her report thus far, and tried to decide why she felt so unsettled about this case—when you read the facts, it definitely didn't seem to amount to much. But there'd been something about the housekeeper's distress, and Javid's painting, and the bad-luck feather that was making her uneasy—although they hadn't the whisper of a suspect, and so any ordinary copper could be forgiven for thinking that this was the usual suicide, and close the books.

She frowned, and then remembered what might be an important point to add to the report—the housekeeper had said she'd been urging Mrs. Waring to go speak to an attorney. As she added it in, Doyle realized that she should have followed-up on the remark; it had something to do with the bullying—well, the alleged bullying, which was another strange aspect about this case. Truth to tell, it didn't seem to Doyle that Mrs. Waring had been living a bullied sort of life—instead, she seemed to be living the life of Riley, what with that posh place and the theatre-people catering to her every whim. The theatre-people were using her famous name to raise funds, the housekeeper had said—but surely that was to be expected? She was the widow of a great man, after all, and it only stood to reason.

And the housekeeper's concerns seemed stranger still, if—as Acton seemed to suspect—Mrs. Waring was involved in the fake-artwork scheme. If she was a knowing participant in the criminal enterprise, unlikely she'd be unhappy about her situation. Unless, of course, she was in the same position as Javid was the last time around, and was being used against her will. Mayhap that was why the housekeeper wanted Mrs. Waring to speak to a solicitor.

Pausing, she chewed on her thumbnail. There was something else Acton had told her that seemed significant—what was it? Oh, right—Basil Waring was known to be attracted to men, as opposed to women. But then, late in life he'd married a minor actress—not what one would expect, but to each his own. Sister Luke used to say that every marriage was a mystery, and there was a great deal of truth to that observation. Not to mention Tricia had been willing, it seemed—had been willing to marry him, despite this. Faith, she'd probably asked no questions, since she'd somehow managed to walk through the golden door so as to live a life of ease, married to a wealthy man.

Doyle suddenly stilled, because she was confronted with the rather unwelcome thought that this was exactly what had happened to the fair Doyle. She'd been a bit timid and shrinking, too—just like Mrs. Waring was—and so she hadn't asked any questions when the great and mighty Lord Acton had proposed marriage out of the blue. But there'd been more than a few ominous things that had come to the surface, post-marriage, precisely because she'd been too intimidated to look before she leapt. Would she have married Acton, had she known what she knew now?

Yes, she decided immediately; and not only because I love the man, but also because—commendations for bravery notwithstanding—I'm something of a weak reed, and that husband of mine is mighty persuasive.

Not that he isn't much the better for having married me, she hastily added—I mustn't forget that. It's been a good thing for the both of us; he used to have his feet set firmly on the path to self-destruction, and now he's much better—he hasn't had one of his black moods in ages.

Her scalp prickled and she frowned at it, wondering if perhaps Basil Waring had a dark side—like Acton did—and that this was somehow connected to his widow's murder. Mayhap that was why this case made her feel so uneasy—there were more than a few parallels to the fair Doyle's own situation.

Because this line of thought was making her uncomfortable, she decided to think about something else and lifted her head to address Reynolds. "D'you know much about the theatre goings-on in the West End, Reynolds?"

"Some, madam," the butler replied. "I do attend the occasional play."

Doyle knit her brow, trying to decide what it was that she was thinking about. "Theatre-people tend to be a bit untethered, I think."

"Talented artists often are, madam. I believe it fits the personality profile."

"No one seemed to think *she* was untethered, though," Doyle said thoughtfully. "Just the opposite, in fact—she was the salt-of-the-earth type, from the Midlands."

"Who is this, madam?"

Reminded that this was a pending investigation and she shouldn't be giving out state secrets, Doyle compromised by deciding that she could discuss the case as long as she omitted any names. "A famous theatre patron died yesterday—a wealthy lady. We think it may be suicide, but she didn't seem all that unhappy."

Reynolds paused to consider this. "Perhaps she had an undisclosed illness, madam?"

Doyle knit her brow. "That's a good thought, Reynolds, but she'd a housekeeper who seemed very much involved in her life, and she didn't make any mention of such."

"Then perhaps the dead woman missed her husband, madam."

Doyle quirked her mouth; trust Reynolds to know who she

was talking about, despite the no-names contrivance—Reynolds tended to keep abreast of all the London news, mainly to see if the illustrious House of Acton was ever mentioned in the coverage. But his remark only reminded her of another odd thing that the housekeeper had said; Tricia Waring did not speak of her late husband.

She mused, "I'm not sure the dead woman was that fond of her husband, actually."

"Oh?" said Reynolds, lifting his brows. "That is surprising."

Aye, thought Doyle; because—from what she'd gleaned—Tricia Waring was not the type to quarrel, or hold a grudge—instead, she was the type who wouldn't say boo to a goose. Her only claim to fame seemed to be that she married a famous man—was willing to do so, by all accounts—and she owed her luxurious lifestyle to him. Strange, that she never mentioned his name.

But nevertheless, Doyle felt she'd ahold of something—mayhap a clue to this puzzle. Mayhap Basil Waring had indeed been involved in dark doings—after all, Sasha Lanska had been involved in some *very* dark doings, and she was a fellow theatre-Russian, even if the two were on opposite sides of that whole Black-White dust-up. And mayhap Basil's dark doings were the very reason Tricia Waring had been killed—someone was afraid she'd talk about what her husband had been up to, and therefore hers was indeed a preemption-murder.

But—as Acton had pointed out—this working-theory seemed a bit flawed, since the strange staging of her death had only brought unwanted attention, which would be the opposite of what the killer would presumably want. That, and Basil had been dead four years already; it seemed a bit late for someone to be worried about information leaking out.

On the other hand, the housekeeper's urging Mrs. Waring to go speak with a solicitor may have been the trigger; it would be ironic, indeed, if the housekeeper's attempts to protect her mistress were what had alarmed the killer enough to decide to kill the poor woman. And this would necessarily imply that the killer was someone who would be aware that the urgings were taking place—a small universe of people, actually, since it seemed that Mrs. Waring wasn't very social.

Lifting her mobile, Doyle rang-up Munoz.

"Doyle; anything of interest?"

"Only that the decedent's money was already in a trust, with much of it being doled out to the theatre every year. But I'm wondering if we should go question Jeremy Grainston a bit more, and mayhap the housekeeper, too."

"What's up?"

This was a bit tricky—since Acton didn't want her speaking of the potential link to the fake-artwork scheme—and so Doyle chose her words carefully. "Acton says the decedent's late husband was actually a Russian named Vasily-somethin', and he'd some Russian-mafia known-associates. Mayhap he was involved in somethin' that got Tricia killed—one of his cohorts got worried that she would spill the beans about Basil's doings, and so hers was a preemption-murder."

Munoz considered this for a moment. "Why would she wait so long to grass-out her husband? He's been dead for years."

Doyle readily acknowledged this practical flaw in her theory. "I don't know. But the housekeeper told me that she was urgin' the decedent to go speak with a solicitor; the decedent may have made mention of that to someone else, and that someone else got worried enough to kill Mrs. Waring before she could do so."

But Munoz remained skeptical, and pointed out, "If that was the case, it is much more likely that the housekeeper would have been the one who was killed, Doyle. They needed Mrs. Waring alive, and if the housekeeper was killed it would have served as a warning to Tricia to keep her mouth shut."

This logic seemed valid, and Doyle said in all admiration, "Faith, Munoz; you think just like a mafia-person, yourself."

"Watch and learn, Doyle."

"Well, I still think we should follow-up," Doyle insisted stubbornly. "I think there's somethin' to all this—after all, Sasha Lanska met a bad end, and Acton says she was a known-associate of Basil Waring."

This was shading the truth a bit, because Doyle knew—as Munoz did not—that it was a Frenchman named Philippe Savoie who'd killed Sasha Lanska in such horrific fashion. But nevertheless, the famous actress had died an underworld death, which did help to make Doyle's point.

"All right. I'll come pick you up."

Doyle blinked. "Now?"

"Yes, now—I feel better." Munoz paused. "That ok?"

"Aye—let me get child-care squared away."

She hung up, and Reynolds—who'd been shamelessly eavesdropping—immediately assured her, "I will be happy to take Master Edward and Master Thomas over to the park when they wake, madam."

"Thanks, Reynolds; if you need reinforcements, call Miss

Cherry—or mayhap Callie; I don't think she has classes this afternoon." Miss Cherry was their part-time nanny who'd already gone home, and Callie was Acton's younger half-sister, who was attending university.

"Very well. Do you have a preference for the dinner menu, madam?"

Doyle had paused at the entryway mirror to give her hair a quick brush, and now made a face at herself. "See if you can work some peanut butter into the menu, my friend; I'm startin' to lose my appetite, and you know how Acton frets." As it turned out, peanut butter was one of the few things that sounded appetizing whilst Doyle's appetite played least-in-sight.

"Yes madam; Lord Acton is a very solicitous husband, if I may say so."

"That he is," Doyle agreed, and then—as Reynolds helped her into her coat—she paused in surprise because her scalp had started prickling.

CHAPTER 7

Munoz pulled up to the residential building's front kerb, and as soon as the valet closed the car door behind her Doyle asked, "Remind me what it means if you've a solipitous husband."

Munoz glanced over her shoulder to gauge the oncoming traffic. "I think you mean 'solicitous', Doyle."

"Whatever, Munoz; just tell me what it means."

As she pulled out into the street, Munoz explained, "It means you've a husband who takes care of you. You're important to him."

Doyle frowned, trying to decide why her intuition was acting-up about this. "I wonder if Basil Waring was a solicitous husband."

Munoz glanced at her. "Why would that matter? He's been dead for years."

"I don't know, but there's somethin' strange about all this. Acton says he wasn't known to be into women."

This caught her companion's interest, and she raised her brows. "Oh? That is kind of interesting—although it may have been just an arrangement; maybe they were good friends, and wanted to live together."

"She was quite a bit younger, though, and somethin' of a nobody—they didn't run in the same circles," Doyle pointed out doubtfully. "They met because he was the producer for a play she was in—she'd a bit part."

"Well, maybe she appealed to him for some reason. She's a farmgirl, and maybe he was tired of his usual crowd."

"Mayhap," Doyle agreed thoughtfully. "The theatre-people are an artificial bunch, and Tricia might have been a breath of fresh air to someone like him." She paused. "Although the housekeeper said Tricia never spoke of him, after he died."

Again, Munoz raised her brows. "Really?"

"Aye."

"Maybe he bullied her, too. The housekeeper seems to think everyone did."

"Mayhap," Doyle mused.

"Tell me what you found out about motive and opportunity."

"Not a lot," Doyle confessed. "There's nothin' obvious for motive—I can't find any hint of a quarrel, and everyone who mentioned her on social media praised her. She donated tons of money to the theatre—it was Basil's money, after all—and seems to have kept a low-profile ever since his death; got trotted-out for fundraisers, mainly."

"Maybe she really missed him. She turned into a recluse, and that's why she never spoke about him."

"Mayhap," Doyle agreed, even though she didn't think so, but couldn't explain why she didn't think so.

Munoz glanced at her. "The Russian angle is interesting. Are there any Watch-list people in her orbit?"

Doyle confessed, "Acton says Igor Denisovich is a known-associate, and so he's havin' a look into it. There's someone with a possible motive, if he was afraid Tricia had loose lips."

But Munoz was skeptical. "It doesn't sound as though the decedent was someone anyone would trust with important information. And why would they wait so long to do a preemption-murder, if that's the motive?"

"All good points," Doyle conceded.

"What do we have on opportunity?"

"Not a lot. The housekeeper had the day off, there's nothin' on film, and it's unclear if Mrs. Waring gave the entry code to anyone."

Munoz glanced at her again. "Really looks to be a suicide, then."

Doyle raised her palms. "Then who's bein' reproached?"

Munoz blew out a breath. "Maybe we're reading too much into it. She was a former actress, and she just wanted to go out with a bit of drama."

"I suppose that's a good point; not everythin' fits the usual situations, and we shouldn't try to force a fit."

"Right. In any event, I don't see much to build a case."

"Aye," Doyle admitted, since this was always the main consideration for law enforcement work; even if the detectives were certain that a murder had been committed, without hard evidence they'd only be wasting their time. "It's always shadows and fog, with these mafia-types. And even if we had them dead to rights, they'd only hire Sir Vikili to save the day."

"Not our problem," Munoz reminded her. "Our job is to build a case."

Doyle nodded, but it went without saying that the Russian-mafia people tended to wriggle off the hook on a regular basis because they could afford the wily Sir Vikili, who was a past-master at his trade. Indeed, his reputation was such that the prosecution would often think long and hard before coming after one of his clients, which to Doyle's way of thinking was hugely unfair. But it was as it had always been—probably since the beginning of time; those who'd money to spend tended to skate on their misdeeds.

Thinking on this, she remarked, "I was talkin' to Acton about how wrong it was, that the villains who could afford high-flyin' attorneys have such an advantage—faith, it's almost as though their attorneys are aiders-and-abettors. But Acton said as long as the client doesn't tell them directly that they're guilty, they're doin' nothin' wrong."

"Right," Munoz agreed. "If they know their client is guilty, they're not allowed to mislead the court, and so they never ask."

"It's all a flippin' holy-show," Doyle pronounced with a full measure of disapproval. "They know very well what's up."

"Again, not our problem. We find the evidence, turn it over to the prosecutors, and move on."

But Doyle protested, "It's everyone's problem, Munoz—at

least the Church thinks so; you're supposed to step-up, if you know that a wrong is bein' done."

"Good luck with that, in today's world."

"Aye," Doyle conceded. "May as well start buildin' an ark."

They were coming into the West End, and so Munoz directed, "Let's keep this short. Even if we think there's something here, there's no evidence and I want to keep a tight rein on the budget."

Doyle nodded in concession; now that she was an Inspector, Munoz had to worry about a budget and—despite what they showed on the telly—the whole point of a homicide investigation was to find enough evidence to get a conviction at a criminal trial. If the evidence wasn't there, there was no point in throwing good money after bad.

As they pulled into the parking lot, Doyle thought she'd mention, "I did a bit of research about peacock feathers, but mainly everyone seems to think they're good luck as opposed to bad."

Munoz nodded as she set the gear shift. "That makes more sense to me—they're so beautiful."

"The Romans thought they protected you, and the Egyptians thought they represented eternal life. India thinks they represent royalty, and power."

"Interesting, that the theatre-people would think they're bad luck."

"Well, the theatre-people think that one play is bad luck, too —the one with the awful wife who manipulated her husband into killin' the king."

"Right. I guess creative people are more superstitious—they're a different breed."

"That's what Acton said, too."

"Pass me a saltine, there's a packet in my rucksack."

Doyle quickly passed the saltine packet to Munoz, who started chewing on it with a show of stoicism. "I'm not sure I'm going to survive this; how can you be willing to do it all over again?"

Doyle smiled. "How'd you guess?"

"The no-coffee is always a dead giveaway, Doyle. And you don't have to treat me with kid gloves."

But Doyle immediately retorted, "Faith, Munoz; that's where you're wrong. You milk this for every ounce of sympathy you can, especially from your husband."

Munoz paused in her munching to smile fondly. "Geary's over the moon."

"A'course he is—men get all swaggery, and think they're God's gift."

"I don't think 'swaggery' is a word, but he does rub my back when I'm throwing up."

"Acton's held my hair back," Doyle disclosed.

Munoz glanced at her in surprise. "No—really? That's hard to even imagine."

"Tis true." Best not to mention that at the time, she'd been throwing up not because she was pregnant but because she'd been shot. The sentiment was the same and so it should count, nonetheless.

Munoz smiled. "You might say we have solicitous husbands."

"That you might," Doyle agreed.

CHAPTER 8

They were interviewing Jeremy Grainston at a franchise coffee-shop because he didn't want to be seen speaking with police at his home—an understandable concern; even though they weren't uniformed policemen, in his swanky neighborhood such a visit would invite speculation.

"We're trying to fill-in a few gaps before we close the file," Munoz explained, which was a tried-and-true method of putting a witness at ease, whether or not it was actually true. "What was your relationship with the decedent?"

"She was Sally's widow, of course, and so everyone knew her."

Munoz persisted, "You were close?"

He shrugged slightly. "More like an acquaintance, I suppose you could say. She kept to herself, after Sally died, and wasn't very social. But you have to cater to the wealthy widows in this business, and so I suppose you could say I was one of the caterers. I'd drop by on some mornings to say hallo, and jolly her along."

Munoz asked as though she were unaware, "How did she meet her husband?"

"She'd a bit part in a period piece we did—played a maid. He met her at one of the cast parties, and seemed to take a shine."

"A bit surprisin', that he'd marry," Doyle offered with a knowing look.

Grainston shrugged in concession. "He'd been having a mid-life crisis, I think. He'd gone a bit moody, and what-is-the-meaning-of-life kind of thing. He did seem happier after he met her."

"Did they marry quickly?" Doyle found herself asking.

"Oh, yes. She was a nobody, and he had god-stature in the industry."

Since this hit a bit too close to home, Doyle hurried on. "He often worked with Sasha Lanska, I understand."

The witness grimaced slightly. "He didn't get along with Sasha, actually—didn't indulge her, and they clashed a lot. Sasha needed someone like Denisovich to cater to her every whim."

Because Grainston spoke of Denisovich with the faintest hint of distain, Doyle offered, "Her husband spoiled her, I think."

Making a wry mouth, the witness replied, "Oh yes—worshiped the ground she walked on. Which made her even worse—she was a diva to rule all divas. Amazing actress, though."

"Have you heard any rumors about who murdered Sasha Lanska?" Munoz asked. "That's one cold case that I'd like to solve."

The witness shook his head. "No. But she ran with a radical

crowd, and tended to be rather outspoken. I imagine the diva-act didn't play too well, in some corners."

Munoz persisted, "Her death seemed almost like a message—a hit with a message. Denisovich has some questionable business connections; have you heard any rumors?"

Grainston suddenly seemed conscious, and replied, "No—no rumors," which Doyle dutifully noted was untrue. But small blame to the man, if he didn't want to open that kettle of snakes; Sasha Lanka had met a nasty death, and he didn't look to be the next in line.

Munoz had apparently decided that it was time to get to the point—there didn't seem to be much to glean from this witness, and Doyle could only agree with her silent assessment. "Had you any idea that Mrs. Waring was so unhappy? We're a bit baffled by the suicide."

He shrugged. "To be honest, I don't think she's been happy since Basil died."

Doyle noted, "It didn't sound like a love-match, though."

"No—I suppose not. But I think she wasn't happy about being thrust into the spotlight, so to speak. I think she didn't like to be one who had to be the face for the fundraising, and glad-hand the patrons."

Frowning, Doyle persisted, "But you'd think—as an actress—she'd be that pleased to step into the spotlight—be wined and dined like a celebrity."

"Right; you'd think so. But she wasn't your ordinary actress—I think she wasn't half so thirsty as the rest of them. And in any event, she'd little choice—many of our most generous patrons are elderly, and they have fond memories of Basil. Tricia cooperated without complaint, but she really wasn't cut out for it—she wasn't even cut out to be an actress, to be honest. Typical story of a country-girl who did well in regional theatre, thinking she was going to take London by storm."

Doyle was silent for a moment—as was Munoz—and she knew they were both thinking the same thing; this story didn't seem to mesh with the housekeeper's tearful insistence that Tricia Waring had been an unhappy prisoner to these people.

Reminded, Doyle thought she may as well mention the other thing that did not seem to mesh in this strange tale. "Would you be surprised to find out Mrs. Waring was holdin' a peacock feather when she died?"

"No—really?" The witness stared at them. "Wow, that's a bit shocking."

"They're bad luck, I understand."

"Absolutely—you never bring peacock feathers onto the set."

Munoz offered, "She may have been sending a message of sorts."

"She didn't much seem the type," he said frankly. "Of course, she didn't seem the type to commit suicide, either, so I suppose I shouldn't be making any assumptions."

"Thank you—you've been most helpful," Munoz said as she rose and offered her hand. In a careless tone, she added as though it were an afterthought, "Do you know who gets her money?"

Without a trace of consciousness, he answered, "The theatre, I would guess, unless Tricia changed things. From what I understand, Basil set up a trust with Tricia having full discretion over it." He paused. "She was always very generous—much of our funding comes from Basil's trust."

"And your elderly patrons," Doyle added.

He smiled slightly. "Yes—and government grants for the arts." He sighed. "It's not going to be easy, going forward; the next generation is nowhere as keen to donate as the last one. I suppose you could say that Tricia will host one last fundraiser, when we hold her memorial service. It's a sad irony that her portrait was painted just in time."

Munoz asked, "Did Javid paint Basil's portrait, too?"

The witness shook his head. "There isn't a portrait of Basil; he wasn't one for portraits—not his style. He didn't even like his name on the lobby plaque. Instead, he was all about the magic of it—the production." He paused, and added rather sadly, "There'll never be another like him, more's the pity."

CHAPTER 9

"What did you think?" Munoz asked, as soon as they were underway in the car. "He seemed fairly straightforward to me."

"I'll agree," Doyle said, since she had the added benefit of knowing that Jeremy Grainston was not trying to deceive them in any way. "And he did seem to think Mrs. Waring was unhappy ever since her husband died—makes it seem that she missed him."

"Contradicts the housekeeper."

"The housekeeper thought she was unhappy, too," Doyle pointed out fairly. "But the housekeeper didn't think she was unhappy because she missed her husband."

"He got a bit nervous when I spoke of Sasha Lanska's murder —did you notice?"

Since Doyle knew much more about that subject than Munoz did, she carefully replied, "Can't blame him, truly. If the Russian-mafia was mad at her, he'll not want to raise that hornet's nest—she died a horrible death."

"I suppose. Let me call Miss Senak."

Doyle listened as Munoz informed the housekeeper that they were on the way, and arranged to meet with the woman at another local coffee franchise.

When Munoz rang off, Doyle sighed. "It's a crackin' irony that I'm havin' to go to coffee-houses all the day long when I can't have any coffee. I'll have to be content just smellin' the smell."

Munoz disclosed, "I can't stand the smell of bacon all of a sudden, so poor Geary has to do without."

Doyle lifted her brows. "I don't know, Munoz. If that were me, I'd rethink my marriage; bacon is the glue that holds life together."

"You never eat anything healthy," Munoz chided. "It's amazing you pass your physicals."

"Now, there's some ingratitude for you; I was strong enough to pull your carcass out of the Thames, thank you very much." Doyle had saved Munoz's life once upon a time, under best-be-forgot circumstances.

"That's all dying down, *finally*."

"Aye, no one's mentioned it in a while—thank the saints; I'm not cut out to be a celebrity."

"You and Mrs. Waring, apparently."

Doyle nodded, even as she mentally flinched a bit. It seemed as though one could find many parallels between the unhappy Mrs. Waring and the fair Doyle, and for some reason, this realization was making her uncomfortable.

Munoz's voice interrupted these rather unsettling thoughts. "What do we want to find out from the housekeeper?"

Re-focusing her attention, Doyle replied, "I feel as though I didn't follow-up enough about why she was tryin' to get Mrs. Waring to see a solicitor. What, exactly, did Miss Senak hope would happen?"

"It must have had something to do with the trust," Munoz guessed.

Thoughtfully, Doyle agreed. "Aye; there's a fortune at stake, and—if the woman was indeed murdered—you'd think that the money must be at the root it. Money's the main motivator for murder—that, or love."

"I don't think love is a motivator for this one," Munoz observed in a dry tone. "Seems fairly clear that the Warings didn't marry for love, and no one seems to think that Tricia was having a love-affair."

"I don't know, Munoz," Doyle replied slowly, since her scalp was prickling, yet again. "I wonder if love is indeed lurkin' about in the background, somewhere."

Munoz glanced at her. "Oh? Who loves who?"

"I don't know. And I think it's 'whom'."

"Oh my God, Doyle; shut up and hand me another saltine."

With Munoz feeling a bit better, they entered the coffee franchise a few minutes later and noted that the housekeeper had not yet arrived. As they settled into a table at the back, Doyle looked about, remembering that she'd been here once before to meet a witness—a young woman who'd wanted to give them a warning —which was, come to think of it, a very similar situation to the one today. And that other witness had been right about her warning; she'd wanted to let them know that murders were being committed to protect a dead police officer's reputation. Faith, that one was another in a long list of cases that demonstrated how good people would nonetheless go off the rails when it came to protecting their own—which was a theme they saw again and again, most recently in Ireland when they were there on holiday.

She frowned in surprise, because her perceptive ability was prodding her a bit, yet again. What? That first witness—the young woman in the older case—had risked her life to warn them because it was the honorable thing to do; in fact, that case had involved a bushelful of honorable people, all of who—whom?—were willing to risk their lives so as to do the right thing.

Which was another parallel to their recent trip to Ireland, when Doyle had scolded her husband about how he shouldn't pick and choose those times when he stepped-in to put a stop to evildoers—especially since he tended to ignore the aforesaid evildoing when it would be of personal benefit to him.

It was a continuing problem, with the old fake-artwork case serving as a prime example; Acton wasn't as much wedded to the concept of justice as he was wedded to the concept of sorting things out so as to suit his own notions. And in the end, that was a sin—the Church taught that it was a sin not to step-up so as to right the wrongs, whenever one had the opportunity.

To be fair, of course, it took a hardy soul to put oneself at risk over something that the law would say was none of their business—which only showed that the people who did so were doing God's work, and should be much-admired. Doyle herself had faced that dilemma many a time, being as she loved her husband

and so couldn't truly do much, except hope she could turn his questionable tendencies, and scold him when he fell short.

Mentally shaking herself, Doyle decided that she was wandering into the weeds on this dicey subject—which she'd a tendency to do—and in any event, the current situation didn't seem remotely the same as that long-ago case; here, they were merely trying to decide if a wealthy woman had been murdered for her money.

Tanya Senak came in through the front door, and Munoz waved to catch her attention. The young woman hurried over to them, taking a quick glance around before asking in a hushed voice, "Do you know who killed Mrs. Waring?"

"We are investigating," Munoz assured her. "But we wanted to ask a few follow-up questions. We were wondering why—specifically—you were urging Mrs. Waring to speak to a solicitor."

The witness answered readily. "Because she was so unhappy, and—and ashamed. She wasn't strong enough, to tell them 'no', and to break away."

"She was giving the theatre-people money from Basil's trust, but she didn't want to?"

"No," the girl confirmed, nodding her head slightly. "She didn't want to. It made her unhappy."

"You said she was bullied—did Mr. Grainston bully her?"

"Oh—oh no, it was not Mr. Grainston. Instead it was the other man—I forget his name. He was married to Sasha Lanska."

There was a small pause. "Igor Denisovich?" Doyle asked. This was not a surprise—Denisovich was just the sort of person who wouldn't hesitate to browbeat wealthy widows. And since

Denisovich was married to Sasha Lanska—was devoted to her—he would have a legitimate interest in keeping the theatre-money flowing. "Did you hear him threaten her?"

Reluctantly, the witness admitted, "No—nothing like that. But he would come to ask about the money, and she always gave in, even though she didn't wish to."

So; it seemed they were back where they'd started, with the widow being rather ruthlessly used for her famous name and fortune, but with no real motive for murder revealing itself. Not to mention that it seemed unlikely that these theatre-people would murder an icon's widow so as to obtain access to her fortune when they had access to it anyway, and needed the aforesaid icon's widow as a figurehead to raise additional funds. And—as another consideration to put atop all the others—since Acton seemed to think this group was involved in the fake-artwork scheme, they would have even less reason to murder the woman, and invite scrutiny.

Apparently, Munoz had reached the same conclusion—that there wasn't much here. "But Mrs. Waring never spoke to a solicitor, as far as you know?"

Blinking away tears, the young woman replied, "No—she was not strong enough."

"Sounds like someone who'd want to do away with herself," Munoz suggested.

"No," Miss Senak retorted, faint spots of color showing in her cheeks. "You do not know; she would say it, sometimes—that she was not brave—and that it made her feel ashamed." Thinking this over, she sadly shook her head. "Someone has killed her, but I don't know who." Struggling with her emotions, she added, "It is so cruel; so unfair."

"We don't have a lot to go on," Munoz warned. "Anyone other than you would think she was unhappy, and decided to end her life."

But the witness lifted a tear-stained face. "No—do not forget the peacock feather. She would never have brought it into the house—never."

"Aye, we can't forget the peacock feather," Doyle agreed, and wished she knew why the mention of the stupid feather always made her antenna quiver.

CHAPTER 10

On the car ride back, Doyle had to agree with Munoz that—unless there was some sort of breakthrough—they didn't have enough to maintain a file, and so all further investigation should be halted. Truly, there didn't seem to be much motivation for murder—and an oddly-staged murder, at that—but there seemed to be plenty of motivation for a staged-suicide, even though it wasn't clear why the dead woman felt such staging was necessary. Mayhap Mrs. Waring was fulfilling some actress-fantasy, and posing like that dead woman from that Shakespeare play—whatever her name was. The one who died of thwarted-love and was floating in the river, surrounded by flowers.

Not to mention that witnesses were tricky things, because they often got things completely wrong, or extrapolated evidence that existed only in their minds; the housekeeper's sincerity notwithstanding, it did seem as though she'd misread the situation. And so mayhap love was indeed the motivator, here; mayhap Tricia Waring never mentioned her late husband because she missed him so sorely—missed him enough to want to join him in the afterlife. A lot of time had passed since his death, but mayhap there'd been some sort of anniversary that triggered her.

Doyle asked Munoz drop her off at the park across the street from her residential building—Reynolds had texted that he was at the playground with the two boys, and so she looked to join them. The usual routine was to take them over to the playground after they'd napped so as to burn off some energy—she wished she'd half their energy, she was starting to feel a bit tired. And soon we'll have three, she thought, tamping down a twinge of panic; I've no idea how people manage.

She began trudging the park path to the playground; it was always an adjustment, going from the world of homicide cases to the world of small children. She often felt as though she'd a foot in two different universes and—as a result of this—wasn't doing a top-notch job in either one. On the other hand, there was nothing like playground-duty to allow for some thinking-time, and at present she felt she was sorely in need of some thinking-time; no matter how much she rationalized this odd little case, she'd the sense that she was missing something—something important.

Therefore, it was with a sense of relief that she sighted Acton's tall figure already present at the playground—he must have decided he needed a bit of thinking-time, himself, which was a happy circumstance; no one was better than Acton at helping her sort-out her tangled thoughts.

He was lifting Tommy to the monkey-bars so that the toddler

could pretend he was going across just like his older brother, and Doyle came over to stand beside him in a show of support, since this was a tough and thankless duty.

"Anything new?" he asked, as he leaned to kiss her—which prompted Tommy to want to kiss her, also.

"Munoz wants to close it up, and I suppose I can't blame her—there's not a shred of evidence that this was a homicide. We interviewed Grainston, and he seemed a good sort—said he tried to jolly the decedent along, and it was true. And we had a second interview with the housekeeper, who admitted that no one was openly threatening the decedent; there were no strong words, and she was readily giving the theatre-people all the money they wanted, even though the housekeeper thought she didn't want to. The only item of interest was that Denisovich was the one who'd come over to ask for money from her, but I suppose that's not necessarily unusual, since he was married to nasty Sasha Lanska and was probably used to strong-armin' people on her behalf."

Acton shifted Tommy to his other shoulder, who made ready to go across the bars yet again. "Did you manage to inquire about the security cameras?"

"Aye; they were there originally, but were removed after Basil died. To be fair, if Tricia herself didn't have any electronics mayhap she was a bit paranoid, and didn't like the idea of cameras in the house, watching her. The housekeeper thinks very few people had the entry code, but she doesn't know for certain, either way. In any event, there weren't a lot of people in and out; mainly Grainston and Denisovich—and Javid, for the portrait." Reminded, she glanced up at him. "Did you have a chance to speak to Javid?"

"Not as yet," he replied.

"Grainston said Basil set-up a trust, and gave Tricia sole discretion over it after he died. But the theatre-people seemed to have no incentive to kill her to get at it, since she was already dolin' it out to them. Not to mention they liked to trot her out at fundraisers."

Acton was silent, and Doyle could see that his attention had been caught. Small blame to him; whenever there was a fortune lurking around the edges of a possible homicide, law enforcement tended to pay close attention.

She prompted, "What're you thinkin', husband? The artwork-scheme is at the root of this? It's hard to see, since Denisovich wouldn't want to kill her for the same reasons the theatre-folk wouldn't want to—he needed her as a front to purchase artwork."

"Yes," he agreed. "Unless she'd threatened them with something—some revelation that would make her death worth it to them, regardless of her value."

"She didn't seem to be the threatenin' type," Doyle observed doubtfully.

"No. I will have to look a little deeper, perhaps—she may have done something inadvertent that created a dilemma for them. The set-up for Basil Waring's testamentary trust is unusual; Mrs. Waring had no background in financial matters. It is interesting that he did not turn over the trust to his bankers after he died."

Doyle ventured, "Mayhap he truly did love her."

"Perhaps. It may be interesting to attend Tricia Waring's memorial service."

She blinked. "Oh? Doin' a bit of investigatin' behind Munoz's back, are we?"

"On the contrary, DI Munoz is well-advised to close the file, based on what is known. However, I would like to observe who attends the service."

"Lead on," she said agreeably. "Never a dull moment."

It went without saying that the unlooked-for appearance of the illustrious Chief Inspector would put the cat amongst the pigeons, if indeed the woman's murderer was in attendance.

"Hallo, Lord and Lady Acton."

Doyle looked over in surprise to behold Seamus Riordan, the librarian she'd met recently in Dublin. A shy, intellectual young man, he'd nevertheless managed to discreetly reveal the fake-artwork money-laundering scheme that was currently giving Acton and Williams fits, and Doyle was aware that Acton had been gleaning information from the young man on the sly; as a whistleblower, it was important that his role not be made public.

With a smile, Doyle greeted him. "Here's a surprise; so good to see you again, Mr. Riordan. Are you visitin' London?" This, delivered with the air of someone who had no idea that he was the prime witness on a massive, ongoing case.

"Yes; I'm taking a graduate course over at the university, so I'll be in town for a few months."

Doyle, who was no fool, immediately assumed this was Acton's doing—mainly because this fellow was not the sort to leave his post at the library and venture into the wilds of London for a graduate degree. Much more likely he was being positioned close by so as to help with the investigation.

This suspicion was immediately confirmed when Acton relinquished his monkey-bars duty, depositing Tommy down on the sand and meeting his wife's eyes in a silent message.

She took her cue, and reached for the toddler's hand. "Come on, me boyo; let's shake the sand from your shoes."

As she led the toddler over to a bench to remove his shoes, she was not surprised a'tall that Acton had set up a clandestine witness-meeting here at the playground. He'd done so before, because no one would suspect that information was being passed along or that plans were being laid down amidst the general chaos that always ensued when a pack of children were racing about.

And Seamus Riordan was a prime witness; when they'd visited Dublin, he was the one who'd alerted Acton to the fact that fake artwork was being store-housed at his library in Dublin. Acton had soon ferreted-out the parameters of the multi-national smuggling scheme, whereby much of the artwork would wind-up on the Continent after passing though the hands of various fake buyers—each sale used to launder questionable money that had been obtained from other criminal enterprises.

But as always, the difficulty with cracking such a case was plausible deniability; even if it could be proved that the players were passing along fake artwork and over-paying for it, any attorney worth his salt could readily argue that his clients had no idea the art was fake, and that they'd relied upon experts for authentication. The kingpins who set-up such schemes didn't get to be kingpins by getting caught-out easily.

And small wonder that Acton was handling Riordan with a full measure of caution; it was a daunting case, and made even more daunting by the ruthlessness of the villains who were operating the network. The ability to launder money was hugely valuable to them, in that it made it much more difficult for law enforcement to intercept the proceeds from their other criminal endeavors. If the Crown could build an airtight case to take-down this particular scheme, it would break the back of many a criminal enterprise. At present, however, they were having trouble even getting a search-warrant; fingers crossed that Riordan would be the key to getting it done.

And in a way, the librarian was in the same position as the female witness Doyle had remembered earlier—the whistle-blower who'd stepped forward at great risk to herself, because it was the right thing to do. Thank God fastin' that such people existed; without them, the prospects for justice would be very bleak, indeed.

CHAPTER 11

Doyle was idly watching Tommy slide down the toddler-slide when she was hailed by Callie and Adrian, who approached bearing coffee from the kiosk. Both were in their twenties; Callie was Acton's half-sister, and Adrian was employed by the House of Acton both as a driver and as an additional security-man. He was a childhood friend of Callie's—since they'd both originated from the town adjacent to Acton's estate—and indeed, Callie had worked from time to time as a maidservant at Trestles. In an astonishing turn of events, however, the girl had discovered that she was Acton's half-sister—Acton's father having been a truly awful person who'd forced himself on Acton's youthful girlfriend.

The previous Lord Acton was long dead, and although the nuns at school had always taught Doyle that even evil people deserved her prayers, Doyle was a bit skeptical about this when it came to her husband's late father—a more awful man never put an arm through a coat, and it seemed very unlikely that even the most sincere of prayers would have any chance of penetrating the fiery lava-lakes that must now surround him.

Callie held up a cup. "Kathleen, we brought you some."

With a great deal of regret, Doyle informed them, "I'm off coffee, since there's another baby on the way."

After she'd heard their good wishes and congratulations, Doyle asked the two for updates, since each of their lives had taken some interesting turns, lately. Callie—who'd been a bit uneven, truth to tell, and small blame to her what with finding out she was not who she always thought she was—was now attending university with an eye toward choosing a career, much to the relief of all who wished her well.

And Adrian was making some bold choices, himself; when they were visiting in Dublin he'd helped to uncover a Viking treasure-trove, and his picture with the excavated find was the one the media had seized upon to announce the historic discovery.

And—because he'd very much enjoyed that experience—he'd now signed-up to take a few courses at university, with an aim toward looking into an archeological career. No doubt this decision was made easier by the fact that Callie was also attending classes—Adrian had carried something of a torch for her, back in the day, and they still remained the best of friends even though Callie now had a steady beau.

Naturally, the university couldn't smooth Adrian's way fast enough, since his face was already famous, he was of African descent, and their archeology department was sadly lacking in minority representation.

As they chatted, Doyle duly noted that Adrian seemed a bit subdued—unusual for him, in that the young man was usually so very upbeat. Teasing, she asked, "What's brought you two to the playground? You know there's every danger I'll put you on Tommy-duty."

To Doyle's surprise, however, Callie made a gesture indicating where Acton was speaking in quiet tones to the librarian. "We delivered Seamus to meet with Acton. And this morning we were asked to help him buy a suit of clothes, since he's going to have to testify in court."

This, said in a casual, cheerful tone, and Doyle felt compelled to warn the girl, "Hush, now; you've got to be careful, lass. Acton's cases tend to involve some ruthless people—keep Mr. Riordan's role under your hat."

"Oh, I do, don't worry—Acton warned me, too. But we visited the shops and got him kitted out, didn't we Adrian?"

"We did," Adrian agreed in a neutral tone.

Now, isn't that interesting, thought Doyle. If I didn't know she already had a beau, I'd think our Callie was a bit smitten with Riordan, here, who wouldn't have the first idea what to do if a pretty girl was flirting with him. Small wonder Adrian seems a bit glum.

"We're taking him over to the bakery next; you should come along and bring the boys."

"Faith, I wouldn't mind a fruit pastry," Doyle mused. "Let me ask Acton if he has any plans."

"Oh—he's coming with; he needs to speak with Philippe Savoie."

"Then I'm in," Doyle said easily, and with a mighty effort refrained from casting a speculative glance over toward her husband, who continued deep in conversation.

CHAPTER 12

Doyle and the two boys piled into Acton's Range Rover, and as he pulled into traffic she asked in a deceptively mild tone, "Tell me, husband, why you're takin' your prime witness over to Sunshine Bakery."

"The pastries are quite good," he answered in an equally mild tone.

Quirking her mouth, she reviewed the street ahead. "I have the strong suspicion that you're doin' a spot of evidence manipulation, Michael."

"There are certain topics Mr. Riordan should avoid in his testimony," her husband admitted. "And some that, perhaps, should be brought to the fore."

She made a sound of exasperation. "Whatever happened to 'tell the truth and shame the devil'?"

"If only it were that simple."

She settled into silence—just to let him know she was

annoyed—and contemplated this rather alarming revelation. Sunshine Bakery had a murky past, being that once upon a time it was ground-central for money-laundering schemes, itself—courtesy of the Russian-mafia—and the place had been put to use for this illicit purpose mainly because the bakery trucks served as a useful cover for transporting goods and unmarked cash all around town without anyone's being the wiser.

The illegal rig had been broken-up by the CID, and at the present time the bakery was owned by Philippe and Mary Savoie, who were running it as a charitable endeavor—the proceeds going toward a foundation for at-risk youth. Which was all very ironic, because Philippe Savoie, himself, was an underworld figure and had been hip-deep in the aforementioned murky goings-on; the Frenchman had originally taken over the money-laundering rig from a rival Russian kingpin. But then Savoie had married Mary, and—as far as Doyle could tell—he seemed well on the road to reform, and content to withdraw a bit from his usual criminal pursuits. Which was to the good; despite his questionable past, he and Doyle were friends-of-sorts, being as Savoie had saved her life a time or two.

And—due to the aforementioned rescuing of the fair Doyle—Acton had granted Savoie a wide latitude when it came to law enforcement. Indeed—unbeknownst to Doyle at the time—Acton had actually partnered-up with Savoie for some criminal pursuits, most notably a scheme to skim public money from corrupt bureaucrats who were themselves skimming money. She'd a huge row with her husband when she'd discovered this, and—fingers crossed—Acton had learned his lesson and would hopefully refrain in the future from breaking the law, willy-nilly.

All this being taken into account, it could be easily be presumed that Riordan was being cautioned not to mention certain subjects whilst he testified about the fake-artwork rig, so as to circumvent any dicey revelations that might implicate the illustrious Chief Inspector.

"You wove a tangled wed, my friend," she couldn't refrain from saying. "Here's hopin' I won't have to bring my pregnant self to visit you at Wexton Prison."

He took her hand. "No—all will be well; my promise."

"What's Savoie goin' to tell him?"

"Mr. Riordan's testimony will provide an excellent opportunity to expose a related rig that is operating out of Bristol."

"The yachts," she guessed. The previous fake-artwork rig had seen private luxury yachts being used to transport illegal goods across the channel. In truth, Bristol had a centuries-long tradition of smuggling such goods, and it was a continuing battle to try to rein it in; there were a lot of boats and a lot of coastline along the southern shores of England. And the yachts had served another, more chilling purpose in that the villains would dispose of any problematic witnesses by dumping them into the channel, just as they'd intended to do with Javid. They were a nasty, ruthless set of blacklegs and Doyle could see why her husband was seizing this opportunity to shine a bright light on their shadowy activities. Nevertheless, she cautioned, "I know it's temptin', but you shouldn't make Riordan bear false witness, Michael."

"It would not be false witness," Acton pointed out. "Instead it would be a suggestion—based on information he has overheard—that would steer law enforcement in the right direction. Riordan would not be a direct witness."

She cast him a speculative glance. "We're poppin' over to the bakery so that Savoie can prime him, then?"

"Exactly."

This made sense; Savoie was obviously well-familiar with these operations, and—as a matter of fact—had burnt Sasha Lanska to death on one of these selfsame yachts, sending his own brutal message to the other brutal villains. And Savoie's assistance had an added advantage, in that if word leaked-out about the source of Riordan's information, Savoie could well-protect himself from retaliation; the other players would think long and hard before coming after him.

Doyle teetered on the edge of mentioning to Acton that she'd the sense Callie was a bit smitten with the young Irishman, but decided it was best she mind her own business. Acton himself had set-up his half-sister with her current beau, and in any event, Riordan was going to hie back to Ireland at his earliest opportunity—Doyle was certain of it. The young man was not cut-out for London-life, and therefore nothing would come of the girl's infatuation.

And so instead, she cautioned, "Callie's a bit loose-lipped about Riordan; I had to have a word."

"Yes—so have I. Unfortunately, she cannot be made familiar with the particulars, and so she does not understand the gravity of his situation."

"I'll give it another go—she does listen to me, on occasion." She sighed. "He's a brave laddie—despite all appearances; there's not a soul alive who would peg him as the heroic-type."

Acton smiled slightly. "I wasn't going to say, but Mr. Riordan rather reminds me of you."

She laughed. "Well, there's a high compliment for the boyo."

"I wouldn't be surprised if the two of you were related, somehow."

"Unlikely," she demurred. "He's lace-curtain Irish, and I'm a shant, through-and-through."

"We have lace curtains, now," he protested.

"You know what I mean, my friend; Riordan comes from folk who lived above the waterline. Not to mention that he's very clever, which makes for a glarin' contrast."

"You are very clever," her loyal husband protested.

"No point in arguin' with you, you're mad as a hatter."

He smiled and she chuckled; it was true—Acton was indeed a bit mad, when it came to his wife, but at least she could tease him about it now, and it only showed you how far he'd come since the old days, when she'd worried that he'd take a flamethrower to anyone who dared insult her. He was much more even now, was Acton, and the population of London was the better for it.

"Da's a hatter," Edward announced, trying to be part of the grown-up conversation.

"Mad as a March hare," his mother agreed.

CHAPTER 13

They walked into Sunshine Bakery, and were greeted by Mary and Philippe Savoie, who were sorting-out the afternoon's leftover inventory; the leftovers would be delivered to homeless shelters in the area as well as to a recycling center in Gipsy Hill, where some homeless tended to congregate.

Doyle's boys immediately plastered themselves against the glass display case, clamoring for the animal-shaped biscuits, and Mary Savoie willingly indulged them. "Emile and Gemma are in the back, doing some cutouts for tomorrow. You're welcome to go help."

With no further ado, the two boys—biscuits in hand—scrambled through the door into the prep area, where Doyle could see the two older children seated at a flour-coated table. And yet again, she thought with resignation, the leather seats in Acton's Range Rover will have to be scrubbed clean. Fortunately, the older Savoie children were well-used to looking after Doyle's two, and so she felt confident in leaving them to their powdery chore.

The older two were—ironically—two separate adoptees; Mary had adopted Gemma, and Philippe Savoie had adopted Emile, and so in a strange way it was symmetrical that the two adoptive parents had married each another. Gemma had been taken-in by Mary during her first marriage, when the little girl had needed to be hidden away; she was a distant remnant of the Russian royal family, and thus was the subject of intense interest by the warring political factions in that country.

Emile's story was nearly as astonishing; he was the son of one of Savoie's underworld rivals, and when the little boy had been orphaned, Savoie had taken him in—mainly, Doyle suspected, because Savoie saw a bit of himself in the neglected boy.

And—equally astonishing—Savoie had turned out to be a devoted father to his adopted son, and in the course of taking the boy to school and to the playground he'd become familiar with Doyle's nanny, Mary, which in turn had led to their eventual marriage and the current situation where the notorious Philippe Savoie was running a bakery as a charity operation and—fingers crossed—stepping back from his criminal ways. Although this remained to be seen, of course; he'd not hesitated to make a burnt corpse out of Sasha Lanska, after all.

To round off the family, they'd a toddler named Hannah—from Mary's second husband—who was currently constrained to a playpen in the prep-room. There'd been a dilemma about whether Savoie should formally adopt Hannah—the little girl's father had been a wonderful man—but they were going ahead, mainly so that they'd all have the same last name.

All in all, the happy little family was a testament to Mary's resilience, and Doyle noted that the former nanny seemed to be blossoming; she'd gained a bit of weight—which was to be expected, certainly, if one were running a successful bakery. Emile—the boy who'd been adopted by Savoie—was entering the stage where he was getting thinner and taller by leaps and bounds, and Gemma—Mary's daughter who was a bit younger than Emile—seemed her usual, rather quiet self. She was an observer, was Gemma, and small blame to her; the girl had experienced more than her share of drama in her short life thus far.

Savoie came over to greet Doyle, looking quite content to be sorting day-old pastries which was a shrine-worthy miracle, considering she'd seen him at his most lethal and on more than one occasion. "Little bird," he addressed her, his pale eyes gleaming as he indicated the shop. "Me, I am the Saint Bernard, yes?"

Doyle teased, "Fah; you're a wolf in sheep's clothin', my friend. You may fool our Mary, here, but you'll not fool me. And I'm not so naïve that I don't realize that if you're willin' to help Acton on a case, there must be somethin' in it for you."

"*C'est vrai*," the Frenchman admitted without a shred of shame. He did not expand on the topic—naturally—and Doyle decided it was just as well, since she was supposedly sworn to uphold law and order.

She also couldn't help but note that Savoie seemed a bit swaggery, which gave her a good guess as to why Mary was suddenly gaining weight. Doyle was happy for them, but she was also of mixed-mind; she knew the man fairly well, and Savoie was not the sort who'd chart a new course without keeping a heavy oar in the criminal underworld.

But mayhap she shouldn't be so cynical; after all, she couldn't cast any stones on the subject of unreformed criminal husbands. With an inward sigh, she wondered whether—ironically—Acton was currently more in the line of a criminal mastermind than Savoie was. It was all very unlooked-for, especially when one realized that this chain of events had all started on that long-ago night at Acton's estate, when—amidst all the other perilous events that were taking place—Savoie had unexpectedly decided to take-in a frightened little boy. So, chalk-up two surprising devotions for the notorious Frenchman; his devotion to his son Emile and to his new wife Mary, who'd certainly changed his life for the better—so long as you overlooked the occasional arson-murder.

I like to think that I've changed Acton's life for the better, too, Doyle mused. It's been a long process though, and with many a bump in the road. Despite everything, the man's still got his demons and they tend to hover just below the surface, ready to erupt—I was only half-joking, when I said he was mad as a March hare. But I do think I've eased his troubled mind—he hasn't had one of his black moods in a donkey's age, thank God fastin'. So, I suppose Mary and I can both say we've been a good influence on what was once a bad man.

Acton went over to speak to Savoie in quiet tones—plotting, they were—and so Doyle moved to join Mary in packing-up the last of the leftover goods. "These look good, Mary, I should ask to be added to your charity-list."

"Everything's going well," the young woman replied, very pleased. "I wasn't certain whether it was a good idea—for us to work together, I mean—but I think we're both enjoying it. And having the children help has been wonderful."

"Everything's always wonderful, to you," Doyle teased. "Just once, I'd like to see you when you're cross."

"I do get cross," Mary protested with her sweet smile.

"No, you don't," Doyle replied dampingly. "And speaking of such, Callie's comin' over—she should be here any minute."

"Callie's not cross," Mary chided gently. "She's just getting adjusted—she's had the rug pulled, after all."

"Well, she's goin' to adjust herself right out of Acton's good graces unless she starts mindin' herself."

"She's young," Mary offered indulgently. "Give her time."

Hard on this suggestion, the bakery door opened to Callie and Adrian, along with Seamus Riordan. After greetings and introductions, Savoie took the Irishman aside under the guise of giving him a tour of the operation, and Callie—who was no fool—watched them in a speculative manner, since she knew as well as anyone that Savoie wasn't an affable tour-of-the-premises type of person. "I wonder what that's all about?"

As this was a crackin' minefield, Doyle chose her words carefully. "Savoie is familiar with some of the people involved in Mr. Riordan's comin' court case, and so he's givin' him some advice about how best to approach it."

Since this also seemed like a good opportunity to warn the girl yet again, she added, "I'm afraid that's all I can say, and it's best not to ask too many questions, lass. It's all very hush-hush, due to some of the players involved; Mr. Riordan has put himself at risk by comin' forward, and it's a hard thing for ordinary civilians to understand—when there's a lot of money at stake, the villains tend to be ruthless."

In a tart tone, Callie added, "And they can bribe people to look the other way, too. Seamus hinted that the people he works for are taking bribes to cover things up."

Alarmed, Doyle cautioned, "Don't ask him about it, lass—I'm beggin' you. The less you know, the better."

With a full measure of disapproval, Callie declared, "Poor Seamus—it seems so unfair, that the burden is on someone like him. He just wants to go back to his books."

"Aye, and I can't blame him. But the whole justice system relies on the citizenry bein' brave, and doin' the right thing. It's amazin', truly, that so many are willin' to risk themselves and come forward. Not to mention that there's the hardest hurdle of all, in that the villains can use their ill-got goods to pay for top o' the trees representation in court—there's nothin' for it; the lawyers can't be blamed for wanting to make a bit more dosh, and the people who have a bit more dosh tend to be the bad guys as opposed to the good guys. It's a big handicap."

"Sir Vikili," Callie agreed. "Viday really admires him, but he seems a bit shady to me."

And here was another crackin' minefield for the fair Doyle to navigate; Viday Gabriel was the girl's current beau, but Doyle had the sense he held many a secret, himself, having once served as an MI 5 officer. Gabriel had connections to Sir Vikili through the Persian community, and Doyle had long-ago learned that these sorts of tribal allegiances tended to trump any other notions of justice or fair play. Therefore, in a neutral tone, she replied,

"Sir Vikili is very good at what he does. He and Acton respect one another, even though they're often at daggers-drawn."

But her companion protested a bit hotly, "How can Acton respect someone who's trying to undo everything he's done—trying to let criminals go free?"

"I suppose it's because everyone involved respects the system."

With a touch of scorn, the girl stared at her. "You can't be serious; the criminals don't respect the system."

But Doyle gently disagreed. "I know it seems strange, but most of them do. It's bit hard to explain, but what keeps everythin' from breakin' out in outright war is everyone's respect for the system, even as they try to get it to work in their own favor. The criminals at the top of the peckin' order don't want to spend all their time fightin' a war with all the other kingpins as well as law enforcement. So, there's a give-and-take within the system, where both sides pick and choose their battles."

Knitting her brow, Doyle tried to explain. "When I was in Dublin, there were rival gangs who staked out certain areas of the city, and then basically left each other alone. When a newcomer tried to horn-in, all the others worked together to expel him, because the gang leaders knew and respected one another, even though they were rivals. It's rather the same, here—even though it's not about city blocks, like it was in Dublin. The players all know each other, and are willin' to keep to their own turf so long as everyone's makin' money. It helps to keep things stable, and no one has to worry about gettin' shived every time they turn a corner."

Doubtfully, Callie observed, "But you'd think if the police

know who's at the top of the pecking order, they would do something."

Doyle explained, "You have to remember the police want everything to be stable, too—not to mention they have to operate within the justice system, and can't just go about knockin' heads together—or at least, they're not supposed to. You need evidence to go after anyone, and the people at the top of these organizations are past-masters at makin' sure their own hands are never dirty. Enforcin' the law—especially in a big city like this one—is a complicated business, with a lot of give-and-take. Faith, if it came down to it, there's probably more of them than there are of us, and we're lucky the villains want to keep things runnin' smoothly."

With a knit brow, Callie's gaze returned to where Savoie and Riordan were carrying on their low-voiced conversation. "Don't you worry that Acton's going to get killed?"

"Every day," Doyle admitted. "But someone's got to go out there and try to keep everythin' afloat."

"You make it sound so hopeless."

Doyle sighed. "It *is* hopeless, lass—we live in a fallen world. So, our job's not to win—that's an impossible burden to lay on ourselves. Instead, our job is to try to do right, and then leave the rest in God's hands."

The girl made a skeptical sound. "It doesn't seem worth it, if you risk getting killed and the odds are never in your favor."

"This world's a temporary place, though. Everyone loses sight of that—whether you're a believer or a non-believer, you're only here for the blink of an eyelash, all the same. May as well try to do some good."

Callie lapsed into silence as Mary came over to join them. "Philippe seems to be taken with Mr. Riordan, is he a friend from Dublin?"

"In a manner of speakin'," Doyle replied smoothly. "I met him last trip over there; he was workin' in a library."

Resting a speculative gaze on the two men, Mary lowered her voice. "Do you think he'd like a new job? We're in dire need of a bookkeeper."

"Why—that's a great idea," Callie exclaimed, brightening. "He's taking classes at the university, but maybe we can convince him to stay in London afterward."

"I doubt it, lass," Doyle cautioned, although she couldn't really say why she was so certain that Riordan would head back to his library—especially if he was going to grass-out his employers in a criminal action. But she was certain, nonetheless, and it was just as well; Callie's hadn't been long in their lives, but already her love-life had been putting Acton through his paces.

"We can see—there's no harm in asking," Callie insisted.

"I don't think we can wait, though," Mary offered in an apologetic manner. "Our bookkeeper killed himself, unfortunately. I feel so badly—if only I'd known he was unhappy." She paused, clearly much saddened. "It was so—so poignant, really; they found him lying in bed, and holding a peacock feather."

CHAPTER 14

Doyle was on pins and needles until they were finally back in car and headed home. At her first opportunity, she'd told Acton what Mary had said, and almost immediately he'd drawn Savoie aside for yet another low-voiced conversation. To Doyle's surprise, however, her husband made no attempt to follow-up or ask any questions of Mary, and he'd said nothing more to his wife on the subject. But now that they were in private, she exclaimed, "Holy Mother, Michael; it can't be a coincidence."

"No," he agreed. "Very unlikely."

"I'll have to call Munoz—she should re-open the Waring case."

"If you would please hold, for the time being."

He lapsed into deep thought, and with a great deal of misgiving, Doyle read him aright; she knew the signs—there was something more to all this that he wasn't telling her.

After a moment, she ventured, "What're you worried about? D'you think we'll need a task-force?" If the CID thought they were dealing with a serial killer, an overarching task-force would be put in place so that the separate units wouldn't miss the fact that a pattern was developing. And all signs seemed to point to a serial killer; oftentimes such a killer left a calling-card as part-and-parcel of their pathological egomania, and this feather-business certainly seemed to fill the bill.

"Perhaps, but I would rather not draw attention to this man's death until I have had a chance to delve into it a bit more." He paused. "The decedent was a CI in the Public Accounts case."

Doyle stared at him, as this was indeed a potential tangle-patch. A Confidential Informant was a person—usually a low-level criminal—who was willing to pass along tips to law enforcement in exchange for payment. Many of their complex cases relied on CIs who kept an ear to the ground so as to turn over information that might lead to arrests.

CIs were another factor in the complicated give-and-take system that was law enforcement—the system that Doyle had been just explaining to Callie. A CI held a precarious position, in that if they were caught grassing-out their bosses they'd find themselves dead as a preemption-murder, quick as a cat. Therefore, CIs were paid well and law enforcement would often overlook the informant's own misdeeds so as to keep the asset in place. Although there were occasions—due to the nature of the beast—that the CI would take the opportunity to play both sides, and take bribes from the criminals to lead law enforcement astray. Indeed, such a thing had recently been exposed in the

Public Accounts scandal; some of their CIs were discovered to be covering for the villains. And it made perfect sense that this fellow had been just such a double-dealer, being as he was the bookkeeper at the formerly-notorious Sunshine Bakery.

But thinking this over, Doyle ventured doubtfully, "I don't know as we can assume his death is connected to his bein' a CI, Michael. Tricia Waring definitely wasn't a CI—the villains kept her well in line, and she wouldn't say boo to a goose. And even if that was the common denominator, no one would leave a peacock feather on a preemption-murder—the victim would just disappear without a trace. It doesn't seem to fit."

He suggested, "Unless both deaths were staged as reproach-suicides, so as to obscure their true nature."

But Doyle remained unconvinced. "Then we run into the original problem we had with Tricia Waring; why go to all the trouble to stage it that way? It's completely unnecessary."

"Very true."

He lapsed into silence, and she could sense that he was troubled. Easy to understand, of course—Acton famously didn't believe in coincidences. Nevertheless, she continued to have the feeling that there was more to this than he was telling her, and so she ventured, "It does seem that Tricia Waring's death was definitely a homicide; we should assume they both were."

"Unless it was a lovers' suicide pact. Any indication of such?"

"No; the housekeeper said she wasn't seein' anyone, and she would know."

Acton continued silent, but silence was not a natural state of being for Doyle, and so she mused aloud, "The feather *must* mean somethin'. Mayhap these deaths were a warnin', with the feather bein' some sort of message. Munoz was sayin' if the villains truly wanted to keep Tricia Waring in line, they would have murdered the housekeeper as a message, rather than murder Tricia herself—they needed her. It's the same situation here; if the villains wanted to keep this CI in line, they'd have done the same thing—murdered someone else as a message, since they needed to keep this fellow in place. So; mayhap these deaths have nothin' to do with the actual victims, but are instead sendin' a message to someone even higher up the chain."

"Perhaps," he said.

She quirked her mouth. "You don't have to humor me, husband. I suppose that theory makes no sense a'tall, bein' as both these victims were indes—spenive—"

"Indispensable," he offered.

"Thank you—indispensable. Not to mention that it's pure chance we stumbled across this one; if Mary hadn't mentioned it, no one would know—save mayhap the field-officer who was called to the scene." She paused. "We should look into the field-officers who were first on the scene—mayhap they were bent, and left the feathers themselves."

Almost gently, he pointed out, "The civilian who found the body would know that the feather was added later, in that case."

She sighed in acknowledgement. "Right-o."

Again, he said, "I will look into this, and decide how to move forward. I hope to gain some insight when we attend Tricia Waring's memorial service tomorrow."

This seemed a non sequitur, but then the penny dropped, and

Doyle nodded. "Because that *is* a common denominator, here; we think Mrs. Waring was involved in a money-launderin' rig, and so was this CI—he was involved in the old Public Accounts rig."

"Exactly," he said.

She smiled. "Look at me; I got one right."

He lifted her hand to kiss its back. "You get everything right."

"Knocker. You should call me to account, when I'm makin' no sense."

"Nonsense; you have excellent insights."

"Comes of eatin' healthy greens."

He smiled, but hard on the comment Edward announced, "Tommy's sick."

With a small sound of annoyance, Acton began to maneuver out of traffic as Doyle looked back to see that her youngest had indeed thrown-up all over his car seat, and was now wailing to beat the band.

"Faith, Tommy," she scolded. "You can't just eat fistfuls of cookie-dough, and let this be a lesson."

Acton glanced in the rear-view mirror. "How bad is it?"

Doyle advised, "We should just abandon the car at the side of the road and go get a new one."

"Don't tempt me," her husband replied, as he parked the car. "Is it your turn or mine?"

"It's yours either way, because if I try to mop up, I'll throw-up myself—the smell alone is makin' me wobbly."

He glanced at her as he reached in the glove-box for the wipes. "You owe me."

"I do," she agreed. "I'd be livin' a miserable little life in my miserable little flat if it weren't for you."

"At least it would be quiet," he pointed out over the din.

CHAPTER 15

That night, Doyle had one of her dreams.

She had them on occasion—strange, vivid dreams that didn't much seem like dreams at all, because they were so real. In these dreams, she'd be visited by a ghost—someone who was dead, and sometimes someone who was long-dead. The purpose of the dreams was usually to give her a warning of some sort—often having to do with a case that she was working on, but sometimes the warning involved an unknown scheme that her husband was cooking-up which was certain to turn her hair grey. And there'd also been a few dreams where the warning had been to step back, and leave well-enough alone because she was only going to muck things up if she tried to interfere.

The dreams were always puzzling—and certainly unsettling—but Doyle had long ago learned that she should pay close attention, because on the whole the ghosts had been very helpful in saving the day. Every now and again, however, Doyle was confronted with a miserable excuse for a human being, and this seemed to be just such an occasion.

Easily recognizing the ghost—even though their paths had never crossed in life—she declared with all scorn, "I'm not goin' to pray for you, no matter what the nuns say. Be off wi' you; go light some coals with Acton's awful father."

"You despise me," Sasha Lanska agreed sadly, her hands dramatically clasped before her. "It is understandable, certainly."

Lanska was the famous stage actress whom Savoie had murdered in horrific fashion, and she now stood before Doyle, wearing what appeared to be a theatrical costume; her red gown copied from a bygone era, and her hair fashioned in two long plaits that hung down past her waist. On her head, she wore a small coronet.

Doyle pronounced, "It's a nasty piece of work, you are, and shame on you for murderin' all those poor people."

"*What's done cannot be undone,* and I have paid the price, surely," the woman beseeched, stretching out her hands in supplication.

"A horrible way to die," Doyle admitted. "But it's not for me to say whether it was well-deserved."

The media had been outraged by the manner of Lanka's demise—since she was their darling—but despite their outrage, the famous actress' murder remained officially unsolved. A few people, however, knew exactly what had happened, and one of them was the fair Doyle.

The Russian-born Lanska had been something of a radical when it came to politics—which was why she was the media's darling. However, due to her outspoken nature, the public had been left with the general conclusion that—whilst her death was a tragedy—she'd probably been a bit *too* outspoken, and had made enemies of the wrong sort of people.

But in truth, her grisly end was the result of Philippe Savoie's going scorched-earth on all the conspirators who'd been plotting to murder his stepdaughter, Gemma. Lanska had masterminded the murder-plot because the little girl was a descendant of her historical enemies; to Laska and her compatriots, any vestige of the Romanov line had to be thoroughly erased.

The plot did not achieve its aim, and Savoie's horrific vengeance meant—in a roundabout way—that the public was correct in their general assumption; Lanska had made a powerful enemy, and had paid a terrible price.

"Easy to repent now, that you're sufferin' for your sins," Doyle scolded. "Be off."

Dramatically, the actress raised her face and closed her hands into fists: *"Tomorrow, and tomorrow, and tomorrow, creeps in this petty pace from day to day to the last syllable of recorded time, and all our yesterdays have lighted fools the way to dusty death."*

"Not a clue," Doyle pronounced, unimpressed. "And don't give me your jibber-jabber; I'm wise to you."

"Just a few moments, I beg of you," the ghost pleaded—again reaching out her hands to Doyle. "I must make things right."

Doyle shivered, due to the sudden, cold wind against her skin, and retorted, "No, thanks—there's nothin' I'll be hearin' from the likes of you, even with all your fancy words. Off you go."

"*What's done cannot be undone*," the woman repeated. She lowered her gaze to Doyle, and pleaded with all sincerity, "You must believe me, I want to make things right."

This, interestingly enough, was true—although the woman was an excellent actress, and so mayhap Doyle's usual abilities weren't as accurate as usual. Warily, she replied, "Be that as it may, whoever's in charge shouldn't have sent you to try to convince me of anythin'. May as well just give it up."

"There are evil forces at work," the actress informed her with all seriousness. "But Rolph is the key to resolving the case. He does not know what he knows."

Doyle blinked. "The Waring case, d'you mean?"

The actress explained, "You must go visit Rolph on-site, and there you will see your evidence." She repeated, "He does not know what he knows."

With some confusion, Doyle considered this pronouncement, even though she couldn't make heads nor tails of it. Rolph Denisovich was the young man who'd been raised to believe he was Lanska's nephew, even though he was actually her son—the vain actress hadn't wanted anyone to know that she was old enough to have a grown son, which just went to show that the woman was a crackin' sink-hole of selfishness.

And Doyle had the unfortunate experience of having to deal with Rolph when he'd dated Callie, for a brief time. Acton had quickly moved to put paid to the budding relationship, being as he didn't need his half-sister to be dating the son of a notorious Russian-mafia kingpin.

“It’s hard to believe that Rolph’s the key to anythin’,” Doyle pointed out. This was indisputable, in that the young man was thoroughly self-absorbed and a bit dim. “Acton will find his evidence without any help from the likes of Rolph—Acton’s always five steps ahead of everyone else.”

“Not this time,” the actress replied. “He had been stymied. But Rolph is the key; you must go onto the site. He does not know what he knows.”

“What site?” Doyle asked in confusion. “The theatre?”

But suddenly she was awake and shivering, even though Acton’s warm body was sleeping beside her.

CHAPTER 16

The following day, after the usual morning whirlwind of getting the boys up and ready, Doyle was walking Edward over to St. Margaret's School and pushing Tommy in his pushchair. The school was within walking distance, and on those occasions when they were on schedule and the weather was cooperating, she liked to start the day with a morning walk.

She was accompanied by Trenton, their security man, and Reynolds too, since the butler rather enjoyed a morning walk, himself. It was a cool, brisk morning, and—once Tommy was resigned to his fate in the pushchair instead of walking alongside his brother—everyone was quiet and content, which gave Doyle a few minutes to think over her dream.

No question that it made her uneasy—that Sasha Lanska was the ghost. The actress claimed that she was trying to make things right—which, to be fair, was something other ghosts had done in the past; wrongdoers had been tasked with trying to make up for their evil deeds. But Doyle wasn't buying what she was selling in this instance, and her trusty instinct was on high alert.

It seemed clear the ghost's appearance was connected to the Tricia Waring case—which involved Lanska's circle of theatre-folk—and which was in turn connected to Acton's fake-artwork case, the one that was giving him fits because they couldn't pull together enough evidence to obtain a search-warrant. Rolph was the key, Lanska had said, and had further advised that Doyle should go to "the site" so as to see this for herself. But what "site" was she talking about? The theatre, mayhap? But there wasn't any link betwixt Rolph and the theatre—not to mention there wasn't the smallest hint that Rolph was a player in this artwork-rig. The young man used to work at Sunshine Bakery, back when Igor Denisovich had owned it, but it was hard to believe that anyone would trust the likes of Rolph with the damning details of any criminal enterprise. Of course, Lanska had said that Rolph didn't know what he knew, which was rather in keeping and seemed to swing things toward the ghost being sincere in her professed desire to make things right.

So; there was enough here to give Doyle pause, in that it did seem as though the Rolph-angle might be worth looking into, and that his erstwhile mother might indeed be trying to make up for her many misdeeds. It would be a huge victory if Acton could take down this latest iteration of the money-laundering rig—and it did seem as though someone was nervous, and tying-up loose ends by staging these suicides. It hinted of panic, in that the two victims were indepsensable—or whatever the word was. Was it *possible* that Rolph, himself, was the killer? It was hard to imagine; Doyle was fairly certain that the young man couldn't mastermind his way out of a paper bag.

But the fact remained that she'd a ghost who was claiming—sincerely—that she was trying to make things right, and urging the fair Doyle to go on-site and speak with Rolph, who was supposedly the key to Acton's money-laundering case. If only Doyle didn't feel so very skeptical about this particular ghost's unlooked-for conversion.

I'll mention it to Acton, Doyle decided. I'll be careful—I know I'm not always the best judge of these things, being as I've walked into danger all unknowing on a number of memorable occasions, and let this be a lesson to me. And I should tell Acton without mentioning outright that the ghost of Sasha Lanska was haunting me—of all the potential ghosts who might be expected to give warning, she's at the bottom of the credible-list.

Although—come to think of it—when Williams had said there was no such thing as a reproach-murder he'd been wrong; Lanska's grisly death was a reproach-murder to beat all reproach-murders. Faith, when you thought about it, Lanska was actually Savoie's second reproach-murder; he'd killed another Russian man before he'd killed Lanska, and for much the same reason—to protect his stepdaughter from evil people. And both times he'd killed the person very publicly—unusual for him—so that even though law enforcement would never discover the murderer's identity, the underworld types were well-aware of what had happened, and would think twice before coming at his family again.

Doyle grimaced slightly, because she and Acton were well-aware, too, but they'd had to cover-up Savoie's involvement so as to protect Gemma from the firestorm of notoriety that would have ensued—one of those dilemmas where the greater good was supposedly served by allowing a case to go cold.

There was little that could have been done, anyway, Doyle reasoned with herself, feeling the twinge of guilt she always felt whenever she tried to justify letting a murderer go free. There was no evidence left behind on either murder—Savoie was too professional to leave a trail—and it was the usual frustrating situation where even if the police were certain they knew who the killer was, the Crown couldn't prosecute a case if there wasn't enough evidence.

But nonetheless, this particular topic always made her feel uncomfortable; she'd been raised by nuns who had a very clear vision of right and wrong, but then she'd married Acton and could see why he often chose to take the law into his own hands or allow a case to grow cold—everything wasn't always as straightforward as the nuns had made it out to be, with the murder-plot against little Gemma serving as an excellent case-in-point. It was the same as she'd explained to Callie—justice was a lot more complicated than it seemed at first blush—or at least, justice here on earth.

Unhappy with the direction of her thoughts, she decided to return to the task at hand and contemplate the reason that she was willing to entertain this particular ghost's suggestions for a single moment; Acton was having fits trying to pull together sufficient evidence to take-down the artwork villains, and apparently Rolph could break the case, all unknowing. How so, though? It seemed very unlikely that Rolph was in any position to know much—not to mention that the wretched peacock feathers indicated something was afoot other than run-of-the-mill preemption-murders. If someone was panicking and eliminating loose-ends, then why leave such a strange calling-card? Faith, by doing so you were only inviting questions, when any decent killer worth his salt would know to leave well-enough alone.

Unless—unless, the feathers served as a brutal reproach—rather like Savoie's murders had done—and so, even though law enforcement were scratching their heads, the intended recipient of the message heard it loud and clear.

Her scalp prickled, and—frowning slightly—she wondered, for a moment, whether Savoie himself would have reason to kill these two people. Almost immediately, she shook-off the thought; Savoie wasn't involved in this artwork tangle and besides, he wasn't going to leave a peacock feather behind, all dramatic-like; he'd think it well-beneath him.

But nevertheless, she felt she may be on to something, and wondered if she should look into this working-theory; find out if the two victims had anything in common that would involve—of all things—a symbolic message using a peacock feather.

Thinking about this, she mentioned, "Reynolds, did you know that the Romans thought peacock feathers kept the snakes away?"

"I did not, madam. An interesting superstition."

"Well, there are lots of them when it comes to peacock feathers—I had to look it up, because of that theatre case. The decedent was a former actress, and there was a peacock feather at the scene, even though I'm told that peacock feathers are considered bad luck for theatre-people."

The butler raised his brows. "Oh? One would be inclined to think they brought good luck, madam."

Doyle nodded. "Aye; so you'd think—what with their bein' so beautiful. But it seems the theatre-people have a lot of odd superstitions—there's that Shakespeare play; the one about the awful wife."

"I believe you refer to *Macbeth*, madam."

"Aye—*Macbeth*." Doyle frowned for a moment. "Did Sasha Lanska ever play that part?"

"Oh yes, madam—many times. Lady Macbeth was considered her greatest role."

Doyle made a face. "I had to read it in school. A lot of people gettin' themselves killed—faith, you needed a roster to keep track."

"Indeed, a very violent play, madam, what with MacDuff's entire family being murdered."

"Well, we're goin' to her memorial service later today, so fingers-crossed we'll avoid any more bloodshed."

Confused, Reynolds ventured, "I believe Sasha Lanska died a while ago, madam."

"Oh—sorry, I changed the topic. They're havin' a memorial service for Tricia Waring, and we're goin' to that." Mulling this over, Doyle added, "By all accounts she was the opposite of Sasha Lanska—no one has an unkind word to say about her."

With a slight air of disapproval, the butler offered, "Lanska was a larger-than-life personality, certainly. And rather outspoken; we can presume she made some ruthless enemies, if I may say so."

"In spades," Doyle agreed, since she knew of what she spoke. "A horrid way to die, though—I wouldn't wish it on anyone." And because they'd arrived at the school grounds, Doyle didn't have a chance to consider why her scalp had started prickling again.

CHAPTER 17

It was mid-morning, and Doyle was driving with her husband to Tricia Waring's memorial service at the Majestic Theatre, wearing her only black dress—Doyle wasn't one for wearing dresses—and wishing she felt better. They'd decided to name their little girl Mary, after Doyle's mother, and little Mary was making her presence known, which made it a bit hard for her mother to concentrate. And it didn't help her general mood that Doyle was left with the niggling suspicion that a bit of concentrating was called-for, in that she'd the sure sense her wedded husband's desire to gatecrash this service was connected to whatever-it-was he wasn't telling her.

It seemed clear that they were going over to the service to rattle some cages in true Acton-style, but Doyle wasn't much of a cage-rattler, herself, and—to add to her general misgivings—she had to figure-out how to bring up the ghost's reference to Rolph without actually stating that the idea had originated from an extremely dodgy ghost.

Acton knew about her ghost-dreams, and he always paid close attention whenever she brought them up, but he never mentioned it otherwise, and she knew that the subject made him uncomfortable. The poor man tried to hide it, but he'd be happiest if her perceptive abilities disappeared completely, never to return again—despite the fact they'd saved the day, and on many an occasion. Mainly, it worried him to think that anyone else might find out that his wife was in the way of a modern-day witch, and he often cautioned her that it was wisest to keep silent, even if it meant that a murderer might go free; it was more important that she never give anyone a hint of her perceptive abilities. Faith, she'd once told Williams—the only other person she'd ever told—because he'd been at risk, but Acton had been very unhappy about even that disclosure.

And so, since this particular ghost-dream was no easy subject to broach, Doyle decided to take the coward's way out and postpone the discussion until she'd a better opening to do so. To this end, she ventured, "What exactly are we tryin' to find out, Michael? Do I need to know my lines?"

Acton replied, "Our attendance is more in the way of a recon operation, actually."

Doyle nodded. A recon operation was one where the police were observing the lay of the land and making preparations for a potential take-down. "Fair enough. Who are we reconning?"

"I am not yet completely certain," was his equivocal reply.

Since this seemed a patented Acton non-answer, she made a sound of impatience. "Fine, then. Keep your precious secrets."

He took her hand in apology. "In all honesty, I do not have a working-theory as yet, and so I am reluctant to say more."

With some surprise, she raised her brows. "Oh? Never say you've made me put on a dress for a wild-goose chase?"

He smiled slightly. "You didn't have to wear a dress if didn't wish to, Kathleen—it wouldn't matter to me."

"Well, you weren't raised by nuns, Michael. The rituals of life always call for a dress—although I wasn't married in a dress, so I suppose I've already fallen from grace in that respect."

"You were a beautiful bride," he insisted, and lifted her hand to kiss its back.

"I was a deer in the headlights."

"It was a close-run thing," he admitted. "I was somewhat concerned that you would balk."

She made a derisive sound. "You didn't give me the chance to put mind to thought; it was all over in a blink."

"Indeed," he agreed.

Proud of it, he was, and she teased, "You'd done your own recon, and knew if I took two minutes to think it over, I might change my mind. So, you kept me movin' along like a lamb to the slaughter."

"A successful operation. One of my finest."

She smiled out the window, because it was true—her husband had realized that if she caught a glimpse of his rather ruthless nature before she'd married him, she might have had second thoughts—although he was a handsome thing, and so in all fairness it may not have mattered. But he was also shrewdly aware that once she married him, she'd stay loyal to him—no matter what she might discover whilst she was repenting at leisure. It was all very well-played, and her hat was off to him.

This did not change the fact, however, that he'd deftly turned the subject from her inquiries about what—exactly—he was hoping to accomplish by showing-up uninvited to this memorial service, and therefore she decided to take a guess. "D'you need me to listen-in on anyone in particular; is that why I'm comin' along?"

After a small pause, he explained, "You are more along the lines of an exposition device."

"Not a clue. Speak English, please."

"I will be given the opportunity to explain topics of discussion to you—ones that I wouldn't wish to address directly with some of the participants, because it would appear too pointed."

"Oh," she realized, as the penny dropped. "I'm a prop."

He tilted his head. "I suppose you could say. Very apt, considering the setting."

But she decided she'd take this opportunity to cast a line, and see if he'd unbend enough to tell her what he was cooking-up. "It seems to me that you're lookin' to rattle a few cages because there's somethin' here that's got you stymied, and you don't stymie easily."

"A fair point," he readily admitted, and offered nothing more.

Remembering her earlier thought, she ventured, "Is it Savoie, who's killed these two? Is that why you're stymied?"

"No," he said, and then glanced at her. "At least, not that I am aware."

She raised her palms. "No—I don't know anythin', it's just

that I can see that you're treadin' carefully—just as you did when Savoie killed Sasha Lanska—and so I suppose it reminded me."

"The situation is somewhat similar, in that I am not certain what motivated these deaths," he admitted. "And so, caution is advised."

"You don't want to stir up a hornet's nest, all unknowin'."

"Always a concern," was his equivocal answer.

He knows something, she concluded, and he doesn't want me to ferret it out, for fear that I'll start speaking of the criminal justice system as though it matters a whit. Aloud, she reminded him, "You always taught me that when you don't understand the motive for a murder, then you shouldn't fash yourself tryin' to find a workin' theory and you should instead just follow the evidence where it leads."

"There are times," he said slowly, "where even in that case, caution is advised."

"Here we go," she sighed in resignation. "I'll be draggin' my pregnant self over to Wexton, to bring you a cake with a file hidden within."

"Hopefully not," was his less-than-reassuring reply.

CHAPTER 18

They arrived at the theatre and were greeted by a young woman, wrapped in a long black scarf and appropriately solemn, who pointed them toward the theatre lobby where several rows of chairs had been set-up before a podium. On the wall behind, Javid's portrait of Tricia Waring was on full display, draped with a black festoon.

They were amongst the first arrivals, and Acton steered Doyle toward the refreshment table. "Shall I make you a plate?" he offered.

"No thanks, Michael."

"You must try to eat more, Kathleen," he scolded gently.

"We already know how this story goes, my friend. I'll more than make up for it in a few months, never fear."

"Perhaps a few slices of cheese," he said, and bent in a casual manner to make-up a small plate.

"Aye, then." It had not escaped Doyle's notice that his offer meant that they lingered in an ideal area to observe anyone entering the lobby, and she tried to decide if her husband was merely practicing the policeman's habit of always facing the entry door, or whether he was more interested in watching everyone's reaction as they first encountered the unexpected sight of Lord and Lady Acton, paying their respects to someone they'd never met before.

A bit of both, she concluded, and I wish I knew what it is that he doesn't want to tell me.

Acton's positioning-gambit paid off almost immediately, as Igor Denisovich entered the room—accompanied by another gentleman—and came to a halt in almost comical dismay upon sighting the illustrious Chief Inspector. In a quick aside, he issued a warning to his companion, whose startled gaze rested upon Acton for a moment before he looked elsewhere, pretending indifference.

Oh, thought Doyle, as she gazed upon Denisovich's companion—a man she'd never seen before. Now, that's a bit unsettling; this poor fellow's not long for this world. The gentleman was only slightly overweight and didn't look to be in ill health, but Doyle knew—in the way that she knew things—that his life was slated to end very soon. Should she tell Acton? Better do so; it may be important—she'd had the feeling only once before, about a sick child, and it had proved to be true.

Acton took immediate advantage of Denisovich's discomfiture by advancing to shake the man's hand in a friendly fashion. "Good to see you again, Igor. And how does Rolph?"

Emanating wariness, Denisovich replied rather woodenly,

"He is doing well, Chief Inspector. Have you met Walter Elliott?"

"Mr. Elliott," said Acton, turning to shake the man's hand. "A pleasure. May I present my wife, Lady Acton?"

"Hallo," said Doyle dutifully.

"Lady Acton," Elliott pronounced in an over-jovial manner. "Your fame precedes you."

"It always does," Doyle agreed with resignation—so much for Munoz saying that whole bridge-jumping business was dying down. To change the subject—and give Acton an assist—she asked, "How did you know Mrs. Waring, Mr. Elliott?"

There was a small pause. "We were—we were acquaintances," he equivocated.

Since this wasn't true, Doyle brushed her hair back from her forehead in a signal to Acton that Elliott was lying—although if Acton couldn't see this for himself, he should turn-in his badge.

"I believe you are with the city's Development Committee," Acton offered in an affable tone, which immediately put Doyle on high alert since Acton was never remotely affable unless he was planning to bring the hammer down on some poor hapless soul.

"Yes," the man admitted with a small nod, as he looked everywhere but at Acton. "Yes, indeed."

"Walter and I have business together," Denisovich offered smoothly, trying to cover for the other man's obvious discomfort. "We are hoping to open the City Quay building very soon."

Acton turned to explain to Doyle, "Mr. Denisovich has purchased a luxury high-rise for development." With a glance toward Denisovich, he added, "I believe Rolph will manage the project, when it opens?"

Now, there's a shot across the bow, Doyle thought; because despite his nasty wife's indifference, Denisovich loves his son and is not happy that Acton had singled-out the young man by name—twice, so far.

There was a small, wary pause. "Yes, Rolph will manage the building—he is a very good manager."

This, said with a touch of defensiveness, and so Doyle hurriedly offered, "Well, that's grand—please give him my regards; I remember him fondly."

"Indeed," Acton affirmed, even though the young man's father surely knew that Acton had tossed young Rolph to the kerb, bag-and-baggage.

Acton then said to his wife, "Rolph has acquired quite an impressive real estate portfolio."

Doyle made an admiring comment, all the while wondering what her husband was about; he looked to be intent on needling Denisovich, for reasons unknown. I'm truly a prop, she thought —like that doctor in those famous detective stories; I'm only here so that Acton can say things out loud.

Any further saying-of-things was interrupted, however, when Sir Vikili entered the lobby. His reaction was more controlled than Denisovich's, but Doyle was aware that the sight of the illustrious Chief Inspector was just as unwelcome to the famous solicitor as it had been to Denisovich and Elliott.

"A sad occasion," Acton commented, as the two men shook hands.

"I was not aware that you were acquainted with Mrs. Waring, Chief Inspector."

Oh-ho; now, there's a bit of counter-needling, Doyle thought with interest. It seems that we're slated to have a polite needle-fest, here.

Acton, as was his usual, didn't answer any questions he didn't wish to, and instead observed, "You wife does not accompany you? I quite looked forward to seeing her."

Smoothly, the solicitor replied, "I am afraid my wife is feeling poorly today." With gentle remonstrance, he added, "She is expecting, as you know."

"Of course," Acton acknowledged in an apologetic matter. "Please convey all my good wishes—I hope she soon feels more the thing."

They're needling each other down to the nub, Doyle observed. And it's all very interesting—why hasn't Acton managed to interview Javid, as yet? Aloud, she offered, "Send along my good wishes too, if you would. I'm sorry she's sufferin', but in the end it's well-worth it."

"Indeed," Sir Vikili replied with a polite bow of his head. "Thank you, Lady Acton."

But Doyle's husband was not about to have his needle-fest derailed by polite platitudes. "An excellent portrait," he observed, his thoughtful gaze resting on the painting that was so prominently displayed. "Although not in her usual style, perhaps."

This was not true—the painting was unquestionably a Javid, and very well-executed despite Doyle's sense that the artist hadn't liked the subject very much.

Sir Vikili made no response into the suddenly charged silence, and so Doyle felt compelled to say to Mr. Elliott, "Javid painted our portraits, and she did the both of us up a treat."

This was true; Acton was very happy with Doyle's portrait, and in turn, Doyle thought that Javid had painted Acton with a great deal of insight; the likeness showed him every inch the aristocrat, of course, but she'd also managed to convey a sense of his humility, too—his awareness that he'd the weight of an illustrious family history resting on his shoulders. Doyle thought it quite well-done.

"My wife, also," Denisovich informed Elliott rather sadly. "I keep the portrait above my bed—it is a comfort to me."

Nasty Sasha, Doyle thought, and was surprised that she felt a twinge of pity for the Russian-mafia kingpin; his awful wife didn't care two pins that her husband missed her so sorely. I wish I knew why the wretched woman is showing up to haunt me—although I'll wager a good guess that it has something to do with Acton's deciding to crash this memorial service.

In a benign tone, Acton asked Sir Vikili, "I was hoping to inquire whether my sister's portrait could be added to your wife's list of commissions. There is no hurry, of course; the advent of the baby is—understandably—her priority."

Now, here's a wrinkle, thought Doyle, hiding her surprise. Acton had no real interest in a Callie-portrait—in fact, she'd the sure sense that if the girl disappeared from their lives altogether, Acton would think it a good riddance.

"I will relay your request with all pleasure, Chief Inspector," Sir Vikili replied graciously, and Doyle duly brushed her hair back.

Rather abruptly, Denisovich said, "Come along, Vikili; we should convey our condolences to the family. If you will excuse us?"

"Certainly," said Acton, who refrained from pointing out that there was no family present.

The three men walked away—carefully refraining from looking at each other in alarm—and Acton turned to hand Doyle her plate as though nothing untoward had just occurred.

Dutifully, she nibbled on a slice of cheese. "You threw everyone off their pins," she remarked, in case he wasn't already aware.

"Good," he replied.

It seemed clear that her wily husband had known that these three would use this memorial service as an excuse to meet and confer under-the-radar, in much the same way that Acton used the playground for such meetings. And wasn't it just like her husband—knowing this—to show up, bold as brass, and put the cat amongst the pigeons even though Doyle was still unclear on what, exactly, it was that her husband suspected. But he'd brought up a couple of seemingly-random topics, and Acton was not one to bring up seemingly-random topics without a purpose; something having to do with Javid's having morning sickness, and Denisovich's fancy new high-rise.

She was trying to decide if she should quiz him about it now or wait until they were heading home in the car when Jeremy Grainston entered the lobby and greeted her with some surprise. "Why, hallo, Officer Doyle."

"Hallo, Mr. Grainston; my husband, Chief Inspector Acton."

"Of course; your fame precedes you," the man joked in a

friendly manner as he offered his hand. "Are you here to make any arrests?"

"We thought we'd pay our respects," Doyle offered a bit lamely, since she couldn't very well say that her husband was here to poke a few bears.

But Acton confided, "I will confess to an ulterior motive. Has there yet been an inventory of the Waring art collection? I would be very interested in making a few purchases, once it becomes available."

Oh-ho, thought Doyle, hiding her surprise; fancy that—and in light of the fake-artwork scheme, this particular topic does not seem so very random.

But Grainston only raised his brows. "Oh—did Tricia have an art collection? I wasn't aware."

In turn, Acton raised his own brows. "It is my understanding that Mrs. Waring had quite an extensive private collection, in her home."

The theatre producer shook his head. "Not that I saw—although it may have been locked away, I suppose."

Acton raised his gaze to glance along the lobby walls. "Or rotated through here to display to the public, perhaps. There would be a tax benefit, certainly."

But the man only advised, "Not that I've ever seen. And besides, it's never a good idea to have anything valuable on display; too many people in and out—we can't even keep the visitors from filching the show-placards."

"If you would all be seated," the young woman in the shawl addressed the gathering. "We will begin the service."

"That's my cue," Grainston said, pulling-out some notes. "Nice to see you again, Officer."

As the man walked toward the podium, Doyle advised her husband, "Not a suspect," although again, she'd be surprised if he didn't sense this for himself.

"No. Is the housekeeper in attendance?"

"I don't see her—and she's just the hired help, Michael; no one would think to invite her."

"A pity," he said, as he ushered her toward a seat in the back.

"Because she'd make another good prop," Doyle guessed. "You could needle everyone to a fare-thee-well."

"My specialty," he agreed.

CHAPTER 19

On the way home, Acton seemed disinclined to discuss whatever-it-was that he was thinking about, and so Doyle tried to hazard a guess; it did seem that he was turning up the heat on the fake-artwork scheme, and the players were feeling the need to meet-up with Sir Vikili for a wargaming-session under the cover of this memorial service. Acton, of course, was one step ahead of them and had made a surprise appearance, hoping to get a reaction—perhaps to see who would now contact whom.

His voice interrupted her thoughts. "Did you gain any insights, Kathleen?"

Readily she informed him, "Everyone was unhappy that you showed up, like the beggar at the feast, but I suppose you already know this. Denisovich was mighty pulled about—you'd think a Russian mafia-man wouldn't get the willies the way he does.

And Sir Vikili didn't much like it when you mentioned the fair Javid."

He glanced her way. "He is reluctant to allow me to interview her."

"Small surprise—knock me over with a feather. Tell me about the City Quay buildin', if you would."

"It is a luxury mixed-use residential development, located in St. Katharine's Marina."

Doyle immediately made a face. "Fah—can't say I have fond memories of St. Katharine's Marina. And—speakin' of Javid—neither does she."

"Indeed."

This, because it was where the artist had come within a hair's breadth of being a preemption-murder. When Acton had begun closing-in on the previous artwork-rig, the panicking villains had decided to kill Javid—she was slated to die by being bound and thrown overboard after the participants had escaped into the channel. Fortunately, Acton had rescued her moments before they'd cast off.

Her husband seemed reluctant to elaborate, and so Doyle made a sound of impatience. "Why were you leanin' on Denisovich, and makin' veiled threats about our Rolph? If I didn't know better, I'd think you were givin' the man warnings to back down, rather than rollin' him up for a few righteous felonies."

Her husband's chest rose and fell. "It is something of a delicate situation."

In all confusion, she knit her brow. "Never say you feel sorry for Rolph—or Denisovich, for that matter; neither one of 'em's worth a moment's pity." Thoughtfully, she added, "You should feel sorry for Mr. Elliott, though; I've the feelin' he's not long for this world."

This caught his interest, and he glanced over at her. "Why is that?"

She shook her head, slightly. "I don't know, Michael; it just seems to me that he's marked for doom."

He returned his gaze to the road ahead. "That is of interest."

"Spill, please," she scolded with some impatience. "And keep in mind that we've two victims, cryin' out for justice—mayhap more, since no one's been payin' attention to the peacock-feather tally."

Slowly, he offered, "I would not be surprised if this new waterfront development is being used to house the artwork before it is loaded onto yachts."

"Faith; they're still at it?" she exclaimed in surprise. "You'd think the blacklegs would try to come up with somethin' new and different."

"It is an excellent rig, because it is very difficult to prosecute. We would need irrefutable evidence to get a search-warrant, which we do not have as yet."

Taking a cast, Doyle offered, "And our Mr. Elliott's involved, somehow. It was clear as glass—the man can't bluff to save his life."

"The permitting process for the development has been slow-walked, and the building is taking an inordinately long time to open."

"Oh-ho," she breathed; "Denisovich is bribin' the Development Committee to look the other way, whilst they funnel the goods."

"Yes. A vestige of the Public Accounts case."

She took a guess at what "vestige" meant, and shook her head. "Faith, but these tentacles run deep; it's like that mythical beast, where you chop off one head but then another springs up to take its place." In the Public Accounts scandal, a wide variety of public bureaucrats were involved in skimming money from taxpayer accounts—not to mention that Acton was, in turn, skimming money from the aforesaid bureaucrats since he could outfox such people without breaking a sweat.

"I believe the warrants-magistrate is also on Denisovich's payroll."

Glancing at him in dismay, she breathed, "Oh-ho, is that so? Small wonder you can't get a search-warrant."

"Unfortunate."

Thinking about this rather daunting revelation, Doyle ventured, "Is that why you were showin' your hand today, so to speak? You want to see who Denisovich—or Elliott—tries to contact?"

"One of the reasons," he agreed.

Waffling, he is, she thought; doesn't want me to nose-out whatever-it-is that he's not telling me.

Suddenly struck with a potential explanation, she asked in an ominous tone, "Tell me, straight-out, that you aren't fleecin' the villains in this fake-art rig."

"I am not," he readily disclaimed. "I have learned my lesson."

She quirked her mouth. "Only because I'm standin' over you, with a brick-bat at the ready."

"Not at all," he offered in a meek tone; "I have learned that crime does not pay."

This was not true, and she laughed aloud, just as he'd intended. "If you ever went completely over to the dark side, Michael, I've no doubt you'd suction-up the entire Treasury, quick as a cat. Lucky for you that you've a hectorin' wife."

"Very lucky," he agreed, and lifted her hand to kiss its back.

They rode for a few minutes in silence, and then she added thoughtfully, "I'd keep a weather eye on our Mr. Elliott—he's the panicky type, and Denisovich may decide he's due for a preemption-murder. That may well be the reason he seems doomed, to me."

"Yes—the thought did occur to me."

With a knit brow, she offered, "You know, Michael—none of this explains why Tricia Waring was murdered. The villains are still workin' the fake-artwork rig, and not only was she a figurehead for the theatre's fundraisin', she was also a front for the fake-art sales—what with her art collection that doesn't seem to exist. Faith, the more we find out, the more it seems that no one would have the slightest motivation to murder her."

"Her death is very puzzling," he agreed.

"And we can't forget that it's the same for the CI at Sunshine Bakery. Why would such an important asset be targeted for elimination?"

Thoroughly frustrated, Doyle blew a tendril of hair off her forehead. "Could they be misdirection-murders, mayhap? Denisovich is obviously worried that you're closin' in—hence this get-together at the memorial service. Is he tryin' to make us think that these victims were the ones responsible for the rig, and that they killed themselves to avoid prosecution?"

But her husband pointed out, "There was no need to kill them at all. Law enforcement was not pursuing either one of them and if anything, the suicides only drew unwanted attention."

Reluctantly, Doyle nodded. "Right. So, not a misdirection-murder. Not to mention that the peacock feather wouldn't be front-and-center if that was the case—that's the oddest thing of all, speakin' of things that don't add up."

"I would agree."

Again, she had the niggling sense that he was withholding information, and so she decided to take the bull by the horns—sometimes if she caught him by surprise, he'd give her a glimpse. "Tell me what it is that you're not tellin' me, Michael."

He considered it for a long moment, and then replied in a grave tone, "I believe Javid knows something about Mrs. Waring's death—perhaps the identity of the murderer. And Sir Vikili is protecting her."

Doyle turned to him, blinking in astonishment. "You think *Javid's* involved in this rig, after everythin' she's been through?" Considering it, Doyle slowly shook her head. "Mother a' Mercy, husband—I'm not seein' it. Why would you think this?"

"According to your witness, Javid came in for the final sitting the day before Mrs. Waring was found dead. However, the portrait had already been completed, and well before that date. The oil was completely dry when you observed it the next day, and an oil painting takes many days to dry."

"Holy *Mother*," Doyle breathed in admiration. "Faith,

Michael; you're *somethin'*—even Munoz didn't piece that together."

"I would ask that you don't make mention, please."

This request, naturally, made Doyle very uneasy. "You can't 'courtesy' your way around this, Michael, even if Javid's famous and Sir Vikili swings a mighty sword. That's a big, crackin' clue, and Munoz should be told. If Javid knows somethin', she needs to say—we've two murders on our plate."

But he was politely adamant. "Please allow me to handle it, if you would. You must agree that the matter is somewhat delicate."

With some reluctance, Doyle could see his point. "Aye; Javid was involved in the previous scheme, and it may come to light that the Met let her off easy. Although I truly think she didn't have much choice, since at the time she was married to her horrible first husband—"

Despite herself, Doyle's voice broke, and Acton quickly squeezed her hand in sympathy. "Let's not speak of him, please."

After taking a steadying breath, Doyle continued, "But all the more reason why it seems very unlikely that Javid would have fallen-in with this new scheme, Michael—faith, she'd be miles more likely to grass them all out, instead. And Sir Vikili would definitely protect her, even if it meant that his clients would suffer; he sincerely loves her, and she him."

"I would agree, but on the other hand, it seems clear she knows something, and that Sir Vikili is determined that I not discover what it is."

"Aye," she reluctantly agreed. "He was able to hide his reaction better, but he was just as fashed as the other two to behold you at the memorial service." She paused, thinking this over. "Is it possible that it's vice-versa? It seems far more likely to me that Sir Vikili is the one who's involved in questionable doings—considering who his clients are—and that Javid is the one who's coverin' for him."

"An interesting possibility. Let me see what I can find out."

He doesn't want to tell me what he's thinking, she thought in annoyance as she gazed out her window. And I suppose there's small blame to him, since this involves yet another situation where he's got to weigh the damage to the Met's reputation if Javid's role in the old rig is revealed—not to mention it might lead to unwanted revelations about the fair Doyle's donnybrook with the woman's awful first husband. Doyle knew—from long experience—that Acton was miles more likely to pull down the pillars than expose his wife to a dollop of misery.

And then there was the Sir Vikili angle, too. Acton and the famous solicitor had a long and complicated history together, and their relationship was a strange one, in that they were often at daggers-drawn on the opposite sides of a case, but each was willing to extend courtesies to the other out of an old-world kind of respect—the sort of thing that a working-class shant like Doyle had a hard time understanding. Indeed, a ghost had once told her that Acton and Sir Vikili were a lot alike and in a way, it was true; they were both at the top of their professions, were involved in some very questionable activities, and had fallen hard for women who had completely upended their lives—they'd been redeemed by love.

But regardless of love's redeeming qualities, Doyle decided that she wasn't going to allow her husband to flim-flam this case any way he wished, and so she asked rather pointedly, "In the meantime, what should I be investigatin'?"

To her surprise, he had a ready answer. "Perhaps if you could interview the housekeeper again, and delve into Javid's visits in more detail. In particular, find out if there were any other people whose visits coincided with hers."

This dismaying request pointed to a working-theory that Javid was indeed conspiring with the villains—either willingly or unwillingly—and so Doyle mentally girded her loins to do as he asked. "Right, then. But recall that Munoz has already closed the file."

"Perhaps an off-the-record conversation, then."

"Right. But I don't tell Munoz?"

"I would rather you didn't, as yet."

"Because it's a complicated situation," she observed with a sense of resignation. "It always is."

CHAPTER 20

Doyle's general uneasiness was only compounded that night, when she was once again visited by the ghost of Sasha Lanska. "All it wants is this," she remarked crossly.

The ghost beseeched in sorrowful fashion, "You wish to spurn, but instead you must listen to me. You need irrefutable evidence, and I know where you will find it. I must make everything right."

This was of interest, in that the actress echoed the words that Acton himself had used. Nevertheless, Doyle continued to feel that this particular ghost's urgings should be taken with a pinch of salt—it did seem strange that she was urging retribution against the man who'd doted on her, in life. Not to mention there was that faint, cold wind blowing.

With a full measure of suspicion, Doyle asked, "Why would you want to grass-out your own husband? Not very loyal of you."

Sadly, the ghost replied, "You, of all people, understand my dilemma."

Oh-oh, she's got me there, thought Doyle.

"I must make things right," the ghost repeated. "Igor would understand."

"Well, I don't understand," Doyle replied. "Why would the likes of you be tryin' to make things right? I can't imagine that you were friends with Mrs. Waring."

At the mention of the woman's name, the ghost's demeanor dropped, and she curled her lip. "A weakling," she pronounced; "I could never abide weaklings."

"Well, Basil Waring must have liked her well enough—enough to marry her, despite all indications."

Again, the ghost curled her lip. "We all thought he'd lost his mind; that, or he sensed death was closing in, and looked for a pretty caretaker. But he turned out to be as weak as she was—worthless little worms; they deserved each other."

"Fah, but you're a mean one," Doyle pronounced.

As though recalled to her circumstances, Lanska suddenly reached out a contrite hand. "Forgive me—old habits die hard. *To know my deed, 'twere best not know myself.*"

"I don't want to know you a'tall," Doyle pointed out. "If you're here to help with Acton's case, best get to it—I'm fast-runnin' out of patience."

Readily, the ghost directed, "Go; go to the site, and you will find your evidence. Speak with Rolph—he does not know what he knows."

The penny dropped, and Doyle slowly reasoned, "Oh—the development site at the marina, you mean? Acton thinks it's ground-central for the rig, and Rolph's the property-manager there."

"*That but this blow might be the be-all and the end-all,*" the actress whispered. "I must make things right; let it be done."

"I don't know why I should do a single thing you say," Doyle countered. "You're like that wife in the play—brimful of evil, and such."

Like a hound to the point, the woman flung her arms wide, her face upraised and her fists clenched in a dramatic pose. *"Infirm of purpose! Give me the daggers. The sleeping and the dead are but pictures; 'tis the eye of childhood that fears a sleeping devil."*

After holding the pose for a moment, Lanksa lowered her hands and smiled rather wistfully at the memory. "My finest role."

"You're somethin'," Doyle admitted, impressed despite herself. "But Acton is somethin', too, and he's a champ at findin' whatever evidence he needs." In all honesty, she was forced to add, "One way or the other."

"Not this time," the ghost informed her, suddenly somber. "And so, it is up to you. *The wheel is come full circle.*"

"Not a clue, what that means," Doyle admitted.

But the ghost only warned, "You must ignore the dog; he is a distraction—a meaningless portent."

Doyle blinked. "There's a dog?"

But she found that she was suddenly awake, and staring at the ceiling.

CHAPTER 21

The next morning, Doyle was seated at the breakfast table mulling over her latest ghostly call-to-action. Acton had left for work already, and so—once the boys had been fed and taken downstairs by Miss Cherry to get dressed—she'd a few minutes to think over what the ghost had said, and to consider how best to address the situation yet take no chances, on the presumption that the ghost was not on the up-and-up.

Lanska hadn't been lying when she'd said that Doyle would find the needed evidence at the site, but there was something here that was making Doyle's antenna quiver—she'd not trust the dead woman until she'd seen hard proof that her motives were indeed pure.

Reynolds was clearing away the breakfast dishes, and so she asked, "What's a 'portent', Reynolds?

If the servant thought the question strange, he was too well-trained to betray it. "A portent is a harbinger, madam."

She eyed him. "A'course, it is."

The butler amended, "An omen. Something of prophetic significance."

Frowning, she considered this. "Was there a portent in *Macbeth*?"

"Indeed, madam; there were several. Banquo's ghost comes to mind."

Doyle nodded thoughtfully. "Aye—Shakespeare liked his ghosts."

"A useful literary device, madam. The ghosts are a form of foreshadowing."

"If you say so," Doyle replied doubtfully.

They settled into silence for a few minutes, until Doyle asked, "Do we know anyone who has a dog?"

The butler paused in surprise. "A dog, madam?"

"Aye, I don't know as we do. Although there's that dog at Trestles—barks his head off."

"Yes—the gamekeeper's dog."

With a knit brow, Doyle remembered, "Mary's last husband had a dog. A nasty sort, I understand—but then he died, and they don't have one now."

No need to mention that the dog in question had appeared to Doyle several times as a ghost, and seemed to be tasked with looking after Gemma, back when Lanska and the other Bolshevik villains were plotting to murder the child. So, he'd been something of a ghost watch-dog, but it wasn't the dog Lanska was referring to because Gemma's ghost-dog hadn't made an appearance in quite some time—not to mention his main job seemed to have been protecting the girl from Lanska's plot, which had been thoroughly thwarted.

"Are you considering a dog for the boys, madam?" Manfully, the butler hid his flare of alarm at what such an addition would mean to his daily duties.

"No," she replied absently. "Dogs don't like me, much."

A bit dismayed by this disclosure, he stoutly assured her, "Perhaps you'd only a bad experience, madam."

"Mayhap," she soothed, so as to turn the subject. "Were there any other portents to speak of, in *Macbeth?* I think there were some floatin' daggers that scared the daylights out of everyone."

"Yes, madam. In the play, the daggers were planted on the servants so as to have them take the blame for King Duncan's murder."

Doyle raised her brows. "Oh, that's right—it was a frame-up. We call them misdirection-murders, at the CID—tryin' to throw the coppers off the trail." She frowned, trying to remember. "Did it work, in the play?"

The servant hesitated. "Yes and no," he replied.

"Typical," Doyle groused. "Faith, give me a straightforward tale, any day—there's far too much roundaboutation in all those stories."

The butler explained, "The servants were executed, but the frame-up didn't work in the end because Banquo had heard what the witches said to Macbeth. And so, he was suspicious that Macbeth had indeed killed King Duncan."

"The witches were sly, and spoke in riddles," Doyle remembered. "A nasty, misleadin' bunch, they were."

"Indeed, madam. And it was ironic that Banquo, himself,

warned Macbeth that evil will offer men a small, hopeful truth, only to catch them in a deadly trap."

"Aye," Doyle said thoughtfully, because this remark was striking a mighty cord; Lanska was telling the truth about leading Doyle to evidence and wanting to make things right but—despite the truth of these remarks—Doyle was wary about the woman's motives. Was she being misled—was there a deadly trap, somewhere in this hopeful truth? It hardly mattered—Doyle was well on her guard, and Acton was more than a match for any trap-makers. So; mayhap she should follow-up on the Rolph suggestion—run it by Acton, and see what he thought.

With a gleam, she informed Reynolds, "You may be surprised to hear that Rolph Denisovich is the property manager at a massive new development—some fancy doings over at the City Quay."

The butler made a small sound of distaste, which was as close as he ever came to expressing his extreme loathing. "Is that so, madam?"

Amused, Doyle offered, "Not your favorite person, I think."

Fairly, the servant replied, "He is still young, madam, and one would hope he has time to learn a modicum of manners."

But Doyle only pronounced, "A fond hope, my friend; he's a chouser, through-and-through."

"I confess I am surprised he was given such a responsibility."

"It's a touch of nepotism; his uncle's the owner."

"Ah."

She considered what the ghost had said—Rolph doesn't know what he knows. Not hard to believe, knowing the hapless Rolph, and so mayhap there was something to all this, after all—

mayhap Rolph would unwittingly give them irrefutable evidence, so as to circumvent the warrants-magistrate.

"How went the memorial service, madam?"

She sighed. "It seemed to me that no one truly cared much about the decedent—there was no one there who knew much about her life. I suppose that's the way it goes, when you've no real family, and you're only loved for your money. It was all rather poignant."

"*Out, out, brief candle,*" the butler quoted solemnly.

CHAPTER 22

Since it was one of the mornings that Doyle went-in to work at headquarters, on the ride over she texted Acton, "Have idea. Let me know when u r free."

"Which case?"

"Waring."

"Lunch @ bench?"

Interesting, she thought; he's wary about any suggestions his wedded wife might make on this particular case. "No salads."

"None," he agreed.

But the fact that he was wary—and that he would put her off 'til lunch; usually he dropped everything if she made such a request—inspired her to text Williams immediately upon arriving at her cubicle. "U there? Any time?"

"Plane to catch, so leaving soon. Come on up."

As Doyle made her way up to his office, she considered how best to broach the subject she wanted to broach. Williams was an excellent sounding-board, and between them they had a good track record of sorting-out some thorny cases. In this instance, of course, it was a bit tricky because she'd the feeling that Acton was keeping information from her and there was always the possibility that—even if Williams knew what was afoot—he would stand buff, and not tell her what he knew about any behind-the-scenes stagings by her wedded husband. This, because Williams—despite his sterling reputation at the Met—served as Acton's henchman, being as he was another one who felt the justice system needed a hard push, every now and again. It was often a subject of dispute between them—rather in the same way it was a subject of dispute between the fair Doyle and her husband—but Doyle could stand buff, in turn; if everyone were allowed to do whatever they thought was best to achieve whatever ends they felt were important, then the meting-out of justice would resemble the Wild West, with whoever had the most clout running roughshod over everyone else.

She passed by Munoz's office—after her promotion, Munoz now had her own office in the elevated realm of the upper floors—and Doyle noted that her door was closed. Just as well—Munoz was as likely to snap her head off as say good morning, nowadays. It would be a mighty blessing when she was through her first trimester and back to normal, where she'd only snap-off Doyle's head on occasion.

"Ho, Thomas," she said, as she entered his office and closed the door behind her. "Where're you headed?"

"Dublin," he replied, as he zipped-up his rucksack.

This was of interest, since Williams was coordinating with Dublin's Garda officials on the investigation into the fake-artwork rig. "Oh? What's up—are you goin' to make some arrests?"

"Not allowed to say," he replied easily. "Is that what you wanted to talk about?"

Torn, because Williams was taking one last glance at the emails on his desktop as he prepared to walk out the door, she admitted, "I'm not sure what I want to talk about, actually. I've the feeling Acton's not tellin' me somethin' about the Waring case—somethin' that's makin' him rather grave."

Williams paused to meet her eyes. "I don't know what it is, Kath, if that's what you're asking."

Thinking of her dodgy ghost, Doyle persisted, "I'm worried that there's some sort of unknown danger-trap, lurkin' about—that there's portents, and such."

He raised his brows in amusement as he shut down the desktop. "Portents? Are you sure that's the right word?"

"I think so. You don't have a dog, do you?"

"Conner would love a dog, but we're not there yet. Things are a three-ring circus as it is."

"Aye—faith, I'm well-familiar with the feelin'."

"Got to go, Kath. I'll walk down with you, if you'd like."

"No; I won't hold you up. I just wish I knew why the man's tied in a knot."

He hoisted his rucksack to his shoulder. "You can't ask him?"

"I tried, but he won't budge. I think Denisovich is at the bottom of it, but I doubt that slappin' the cuffs on Denisovich would be makin' him grave. There's somethin' more afoot."

He nodded, and opened the door for her. "If I find out anything that I can tell you, I will. How's that?"

"I appreciate it, my friend. Go, and give my regards to the banshees. I'll see if Munoz can tell me anythin' of interest."

He lowered his voice as they stepped into the hallway. "Munoz is lying down in her office, and Lizzie is fielding her calls."

Lizzie being Williams' wife, who usually worked in the forensics lab. Doyle made a sound of sympathy. "Poor Munoz; I wonder if she'll have to take some time off?"

"She should, but she's stubborn. She needs to learn that some things are more important than others."

Doyle had to smile. "Never thought I'd hear the likes of you sayin' that, Thomas Williams."

"I say it to Lizzie practically every day, but it falls on deaf ears." This said as he glanced over at her with some significance; Lizzie originated from Acton's hereditary estate, and was even more of an Acton-henchman than Williams was.

Doyle assured him, "Say no more; I'll see if I can get Acton to ease-off poor Lizzie. This balancing-family-and-work is not for the faint of heart, and its lucky that you've no idea, goin' in."

"I'd appreciate it—got to go."

"Good luck to you, my friend."

He strode away down the hallway as Doyle lingered outside Munoz's closed office door. After debating whether to go in for a moment, she decided she'd go prime Acton's assistant for information, instead.

She walked over to Nazy's desk, which was situated in the hallway outside of Acton's office. The young Persian woman was at her post, competently handling her busy desk; Nazy was ideally suited for the job—organized and efficient, even as she was not someone who tended to put two and two together, which was precisely why Acton had chosen her to be his assistant. That, and she was unlikely to try to murder people so as to go after her boss, like the last assistant had.

"Ho, Nazy; I came by to see Munoz, but her door's firmly shut."

Nazy glanced over toward Munoz's office and lowered her voice. "I think she is resting, Officer Doyle; she has not been feeling well."

"Katy bar the door," Doyle joked.

The girl frowned in confusion. "No—I believe it is Lizzie Williams who is in there with her."

"Ah," said Doyle. "My mistake." She then asked in a casual manner, "What's the status of the Tricia Waring case, d'you know? It would save me havin' to beard the Munoz-lion in her den."

"Oh—I believe that case is closed, Officer Doyle."

"Was it listed as misadventure or suicide?" All non-homicide deaths that were not from natural causes were required to be categorized one way or the other.

Nazy typed a few keys and pulled up the report. "Suicide, it says."

"Does it? Then I suppose the peacock feather was just for show, after all."

Nazy frowned in confusion. "Peacock feather?"

For reasons which were unclear, Doyle was not a'tall surprised that her husband had deleted this interesting tidbit from the final report. "Aye; the decedent was holding a peacock feather—very poignant," Doyle offered, very pleased that she was given yet another chance to use the ten-pound word. "Although I suppose that's not always the case; your people think they mean royalty, or somethin'—there's that peacock throne."

Nazy pressed her lips together briefly. "The peacock throne is India, Officer Doyle, not Pakistan."

Yikes, put my foot in it there, thought Doyle. "Oh—sorry, Nazy; no offense."

Nazy unbent enough to explain, "In fact, the Persian people do not honor peacocks at all, Officer Doyle—there is a famous fable about them. They used to have the sweetest voice of all the birds, but then they fell from grace. That is why they screech so; because they are damned."

Fascinated, Doyle asked, "Is that so? Faith, how did they fall from grace?"

Nazy advised with all earnestness, "The peacock helped the serpent, when it tricked Eve into eating the forbidden fruit."

"A vile aider-and-abettor," Doyle pronounced. "Shouldn't try to trump God—that's a losin' fight."

Nazy nodded wisely. "Indeed, Officer Doyle."

Thinking about this, Doyle mused, "Fancy that; peacocks are villains in your culture—just like they are for the theatre-people, but everyone else seems to think they're the top o' the trees."

"It is only a fable, Officer Doyle," Nazy demurred with a smile. "I don't think anyone pays attention to such things anymore."

Someone is, thought Doyle; and it's mighty interesting that my husband left this little factor out of the official report.

Doyle's mobile pinged, and she said, "Oh—here's Munoz—speak o' the devil and up she pops. Let me see what she wants."

Doyle then answered the call in her best support-officer voice, "Ma'am."

"Doyle; Dispatch says Grainston from the theatre is dead on the premises. Cause of death is unclear."

"Holy *Mother*," breathed Doyle in astonishment. "Now, isn't *that* a wrinkle?"

"Can you assist?"

"I'm right outside your door, talkin' to Nazy." Doyle paused. "How're you doin'? I'll cover it for you, if you need me to."

"No, I'm all right. Williams is out of jurisdiction, so the SIO will be Gabriel."

"Ready when you are," Doyle said, and rang off.

"Mother a' Mercy; here's a surprise," she said to Nazy. "Got to go—needs must, when the devil drives."

Discreetly aghast, Nazy gently chided, "I don't think Officer Munoz qualifies as a *devil*, Officer Doyle."

"You'd be surprised, my friend," Doyle observed darkly.

CHAPTER 23

In a matter of minutes, Doyle was once again seated in Munoz's unmarked vehicle and driving over to the West End. "What do we know?"

"Not a lot. Dispatch says he was found at the theatre less than an hour ago. The field-officer says he was there to meet with a production team to talk about a new play. Before the meeting started, he went backstage to make coffee and never came back, so they went to look for him. He was lying in the hallway—possible heart attack. They called me because he's already in the database as a witness in the Tricia Waring death."

"Seems mighty smoky," Doyle observed. "We should take a long look at the coffee."

"Coffee was spilled, nothing remains. The cup's been bagged and tagged." Munoz glanced at Doyle. "I informed Acton, and he wants to come have a look. He's got something going on with Williams, and then he'll be over."

"Aye; I think they're linin' up a take-down on the fake-artwork case. Williams is off to Dublin to help coordinate."

"Any idea why Acton's interested in Grainston?"

Doyle weighed what to say, and then decided to disclose, "I think he thinks Mrs. Waring's death is connected to the artwork-rig. She's a known-associate of Igor Denisovich, and he thinks Denisovich is up to his neck in it."

Munoz frowned slightly, thinking this over. "And now Grainston and Mrs. Waring are both dead, just as Acton is moving-in over in Dublin."

"Oh," Doyle said with raised brows. "Now, there's a good point."

"Denisovich may be panicking—these may be preemption-murders, with these two victims as low-level players."

"Mayhap," Doyle agreed aloud, but—even though this was a plausible working-theory—she knew, in the way that she knew things, that such was not the case. Doyle had spoken to Grainston on two occasions, now, and was left with the impression that the man had nothing to hide. Of course, this was not something she could tell Munoz, which meant it was her usual dilemma; she'd lay the whole before Acton, and let him decide what to do. Not that she'd much confidence that he'd actually follow through; he knew something, and didn't want whatever-it-was to see the light of day. But in the meantime, the bodies were hitting the floor and it was enough to make you swear-off marriage.

And speaking of such, Doyle eyed her companion and ventured, "How're you feelin', then?"

"Better. Lizzie Williams gave me something, and I think it's working."

"A potion?" Doyle asked with some alarm.

"No, some concoction of mint and ginger—low-doses of various herbs. She said she was experimenting when she was pregnant, and came up with it."

Doyle raised her brows. "If she can find a cure for mornin' sickness, my hat's off to her."

"Amen to that."

They arrived at the theatre, where the field-officer was on the lookout and directed them toward a taped-off hallway.

"Let's have a look," Munoz said, pulling on her gloves.

"Yes, ma'am. Follow me."

The two detectives followed the PC into the narrow hallway behind the theatre's stage—the hallway containing multiple doors that led into various dressing rooms, and a few storage closets. The walls were old and battered, and gave off the faint scent of dust and perfume; the only lighting consisted of old-school exposed light bulbs, overhead.

Jeremy Grainston was lying near a wall, and he was crumpled in a position that indicated he'd collapsed whilst trying to brace himself against it.

So; not a staged-suicide like the others, Doyle thought. But it's hard to believe that this is just a coincidence.

Munoz reviewed the scene. "Do we have his mobile?"

"I haven't moved him yet, ma'am—waiting for you."

Munoz nodded, and asked Doyle to take some photographs before they moved the body into a position more conducive to a search. As Doyle was taking her snaps from various angles, Officer Gabriel approached them down the hall. "Good morning, detectives; what have we here?"

"Looks to be a sudden collapse, sir," Munoz said. "He was a witness one of my cases, and so we were called-in; we were just getting ready to look for a mobile."

"Then let me help you lay him out, Inspector," said Gabriel.

Doyle inwardly winced at how formal they were with one another; Munoz and Gabriel had been romantically involved, once upon a time, and it always seemed to Doyle that Gabriel still harbored feelings for the fair Munoz. It was water well-under the bridge, of course; Munoz had married her husband, and Gabriel was involved with Acton's half-sister, Callie. Nevertheless, she could sense his longing—carefully hidden away—and it made her rather sad—a shame, that everyone didn't wind-up with who they wanted to, but some things weren't meant to be and there was no point in second-guessing; in all things, give thanks.

Their manner strictly professional, the two gently repositioned the decedent onto his back. Grainston was wearing a jacket, and Munoz carefully unzipped it so as to check his inner pockets. As she did so, her actions exposed a single peacock feather resting atop his white shirt, its trailing tendrils a bit squashed but nonetheless shining beautifully iridescent, in the light from the single bulb overhead.

There was a moment's profound silence. "Holy Mother," said Doyle.

"What?" Gabriel asked, his tone sharp.

Munoz explained, "In the original case—suicide of a theatre patron—the woman was holding a peacock feather." She turned to Doyle and directed, "Let's take some film."

As Doyle lifted her tablet to record, Munoz explained, "It

might be a calling-card. These may be preemption-murders in one of DCI Acton's cases—the artwork money-laundering one."

Gabriel whistled softly. "Wow. Then we're witnessing a touch of panic, perhaps."

"Mayhap," Doyle agreed aloud, even though her own sure sense was telling her that Grainston had not been involved in the scheme. She teetered on the edge of mentioning the peacock-feather CI at Sunshine Bakery, but decided she'd best button her lip and speak with Acton before she said anything further—he may not be best-pleased to have that development disclosed to Munoz and Gabriel; not that they couldn't be trusted, but this case was proving to be a hard nut to crack, and the tighter the lid, the better.

And so instead, she asked, "D'you want me to interview the reportin' witness?"

"I'll come too," Munoz decided, and the two of them left Gabriel to wait for the Coroner whilst they walked down to the other end of the hallway, where another field officer was guarding the taped perimeter. The reporting witness—a young man who was seated on a folding chair—was looking into his mobile with an air of boredom, but when he saw them approaching, he brightened a bit. "Oh—you're that police officer, aren't you? The bridge-jumper."

"I am," Doyle affirmed.

"Could I take a snap?"

"Later," said Munoz rather brusquely, since morning-sickness could strike at any moment and she was annoyed by the resurrection of this topic. "Right now, we need to interview you. Why were you here this morning?"

The young man blew out a breath. "I'm an ASM for the new production."

"Which means?"

"I'm one of the assistant stage managers—the stage manager gives us various tasks to help him get the production on track. I'm lower on the totem-pole, so I was asked to handle this assignment—fetch coffee or whatever, while the production people discuss what's needed on the project."

Alert, Munoz asked, "If you were here to fetch coffee, why did Mr. Grainston go to make his own?"

The young man looked at them in surprise. "Did he? I thought he came in with his own coffee; it was a cannister from home, I think."

Munoz and Doyle were silent for a moment, processing the interesting fact that somehow, the cannister had disappeared and instead a plain paper coffee cup had been bagged as evidence. Doyle made a note on her tablet to check CCTV video so as to verify whether the man was carrying a cannister when he entered the building.

Munoz asked, "Where was the production meeting?"

"In the theatre seats—they'll want to talk about backdrops, and staging."

"Who was there?"

The young man rattled off a list of six people as Doyle entered their names in her tablet. He then concluded, "That's everyone; Jeremy was knocking about back stage and we were waiting for him." He paused. "When he didn't appear, they asked me to go rout him out." He paused, turning somber at the memory. "Gave me a fright, I'll say. I called the police."

They were silent for a moment, assessing the witness, and then Munoz asked, "Do you know if he was upset about anything?"

"No—but I never talked to him much. I'm too low on the totem-pole."

Doyle asked, "Was he quarrelin' with anyone who was here? Have you heard any gossip?"

The witness shrugged. "No; everyone liked him—or at least, they respected him. He got things done, which is not easy when you're dealing with all the big egos."

Munoz asked, "Any surveillance film we can review?"

"Oh, no—that's a definite no-no. No actor wants cameras backstage."

Doyle decided she may as well ask, "D'you know if there were any peacock feathers on the premises?"

The young man looked at her in surprise. "Never—peacock feathers are bad luck," he explained, with the air of someone disclosing an irrefutable fact.

CHAPTER 24

They returned to Grainston's body, and when Munoz stepped aside to phone-in a preliminary report to Acton, Doyle noted that Gabriel's gaze lingered on the young woman, now that her back was turned. Faith, she thought with a pang; he loves her still, and mayhap he always will. I should thank God fastin' that Acton threw me across his saddle-bow and put paid to any notion of a courtship; this love and longin' business is for the birds.

In case he didn't know, Doyle informed Gabriel, "I think DCI Acton's comin' in to have a look."

Gabriel glanced at her. "Is he? We'd best put on a good front, then—try to look busy."

Not certain of how much he was aware, Doyle nevertheless thought it safe to say, "Williams was the SIO on the Waring case, but he's goin' to Dublin, so that's why you've been pulled-in."

Gabriel cocked his head. "I hope Williams will be careful;

Dublin's not a healthy place to be—they're coshing solicitors on the streets."

This, because when Doyle had been holidaying with her family in Dublin, a solicitor from the same Inns of Court as Sir Vikili had met an untimely death. Lisa Davies had been a brash woman who'd decided she could outfox the illustrious Chief Inspector, and had come to a bad end as the inevitable result of such thinking.

"Such a shame," Doyle replied in a neutral tone, and wondered how much Gabriel knew about what had happened. Come to think of it, she seemed to recall that the dead woman said she'd dined with Sir Vikili, Javid, and Gabriel just before she'd come to Dublin—not that Gabriel or Sir Vikili would help someone like Lisa Davies scheme against the House of Acton, of course; they knew better.

She ventured, "You may have been one of the last to see her alive, I think—there was a dinner-party or somethin' that she spoke of."

He grimaced. "Don't remind me; I thought Vikili was going to come to blows with her."

Assuming that Sir Vikili had been trying to warn Davies not to pull at Acton's tail, Doyle feigned ignorance and raised her brows. "Truly? I thought Sir Vikili was somethin' of a mentor to her."

But her companion went a different way than Doyle had anticipated. "Vikili's very protective of his wife, and Davies was practically sneering at her. It made for a very uncomfortable meal."

Blinking in surprise, Doyle exclaimed, "Faith, why on earth would Lisa Davies be sneerin' at Javid?"

He shrugged slightly. "Javid's been trying to convince Vikili to sign-up for the Indigent Defense Fund."

He gave her a look, and Doyle couldn't help but smile. The Indigent Defense Fund was an organization of private criminal defense attorneys who volunteered to represent indigent defendants—the premise being that the attorneys appointed courtesy of the Crown weren't always of the highest quality, and indigent defendants should be afforded premiere representation, too.

Doyle observed, "Well, Javid may be on the side of the angels, but she's whistlin' in the wind; that's never goin' to happen."

"You and the late Lisa Davies are in agreement, then."

Wincing slightly, Doyle countered, "Save that I'd never sneer at Javid—and especially in front of her husband. It stands to reason that Davies would, though; she was somethin' of a needler—didn't know when to pull-in her horns."

"Exactly. Lucky that she died in Dublin, or I'd be in danger of suspecting that Vikili was the one who coshed her."

Best change the subject, Doyle decided, since the subject of who'd-coshed-Lisa-Davies was one she should probably avoid. "D'you think you'll call-in a SOCO team here?"

"I'll wait for his lordship to make an appearance, and give us a hint of how he wishes to proceed. It doesn't help that the area is not conducive to forensics—too many people in and out."

"Aye, and there are no cameras backstage," she added. "Not a lot to go on, unless we can get somethin' concrete on the switched coffee." She lowered her gaze to the remains of Jeremy

Grainston, and the incongrous feather that rested on his chest. "He'll definitely have electronics, though. Waring—the last peacock-feather victim—didn't."

"There's no mobile on him, which seems a little odd," Gabriel pointed out.

"The killer may have taken it. We can always subpoena the records."

But Gabriel was skeptical. "There's no guarantee they'll be much help, though. He was here on other business, so unlikely there's a communication from a potential killer, asking him to meet for a switch of coffee-cups."

"A good point. I've a feelin' we'll be left clutchin' at straws, same as the other deaths connected to this poor theatre; first Waring, now Grainston, and—lest we forget—Sasha Lanska, who started the ball rollin'."

Gabriel's attention suddenly sharpened. "Does Acton think there might be a connection to Lanska's death? Denisovich was her husband—maybe this is just an old-fashioned turf-war, between rival mafia interests."

"I'm not sure what he thinks," Doyle replied, which was true. "But a mafia-war seems unlikely to me—these victims don't seem to have been key players in any Denisovich goings-on. Instead they're just perip—perenfabal—"

"Peripheral," he supplied.

"Thank you—peripheral people, as far as I can see. For the same reason, it's unlikely they're preemption-murders by Denisovich, since he definitely wouldn't have killed his wife, and he needed Tricia Waring for her money. And Grainston wasn't involved a'tall, I think."

Gabriel's gaze rested thoughtfully upon the feather. "But they've something in common, obviously."

"Aye," she conceded. "I wish I knew what it was."

They heard voices down the hall, and looked up to see Acton walking toward them with Munoz, the two having a low-voiced conversation. After greeting them, the DCI reviewed Grainston's body, and Doyle was suddenly made aware that her husband wasn't a'tall surprised by this latest death.

And meanwhile, I'm as gob-smacked as can be, she thought with a full measure of annoyance. I've been patient long enough, and it's past time to put the man in a chokehold to force him to tell me what's afoot.

As the four detectives silently contemplated the scene, Gabriel offered, "Seems odd he had the feather tucked into his belt. He'd an empty hand—why wasn't he carrying it?"

"A good question," Doyle husband replied, and Doyle had to resist giving him a sharp glance, because this was a lie.

Gabriel continued, "If it was a fetish, you'd think he would have carried it under his shirt."

Acton made no comment—no doubt having realized that his wife wasn't buying what he was selling—and Munoz pointed out, "Maybe he hid it because he didn't want anyone to know he had it; they're supposed to be bad luck."

With some surprise, Gabriel observed, "But none of these people are Persian."

Oh, Doyle realized; Gabriel's half-Persian, and he must be thinking of Nazy's fable. She explained, "They're bad luck for the theatre-people, too. It's a theatre superstition, just like that Scottish play."

"*Macbeth*?" Gabriel asked, his dark brows raised. "I will admit I was not expecting a literary reference from you, Detective Sergeant."

"It may be more appropriate than you think," she insisted. "Mayhap these peacock-feathers are an attempt at misdirection—just like in the play, when they tried to pin the murder on the servants." Warming to this idea, she added, "It would help explain why these victims were chosen even though they weren't major players. Mayhap someone is tryin' to throw dust in our eyes, with this whole feathers holy-show."

Acton nodded. "I think it warrants a SOCO team, Inspector—I don't hold out much hope, but perhaps they can isolate something useful."

Munoz nodded. "Very good, sir."

Doyle was hard-pressed not to glance at him again, because she knew, in the way that she knew things, that Acton held the sure knowledge that the forensics team would find nothing of interest.

Her husband then advised her, "If you would review the CCTV footage from the street-view, Sergeant."

"Yes, sir."

Munoz added, "I'll go to his home, and supervise a search. His electronics may be helpful."

"Indeed," Acton agreed, and Doyle kept her face lowered, since she was once again aware that he'd no hope of such a thing.

CHAPTER 25

Once they were in the Range Rover, Doyle tried to keep her voice neutral despite her mounting impatience with her exasperating husband. "It seems as though the victim's coffee was spiked in some way, and then the killer substituted another cup."

"I would agree."

"But it makes no sense, Michael; Grainston wasn't involved in the artwork-rig—not a'tall. He was tellin' the truth when he said he knew nothin' about Tricia Waring's death, same as when he said he knew nothin' about her supposed artwork collection. So—someone's tryin' to implicate him, but he's clean as a whistle—or he was, poor man."

"Indeed."

Unable to maintain her neutral tone, she chided, "I recognize that 'indeed', my friend; it's the kind of 'indeed' you say when you're buttonin' your lip and hopin' I don't get a glimpse into what you're thinkin'. You know somethin', and I'd like to hear whatever-it-is, if you please. We're supposed to be pursuin' justice, here."

After a slight pause—no doubt weighing his marital options—he offered, "I believe your theory is the correct one; Grainston's death is a misdirection-murder."

Readily, she nodded. "Aye. I think he's bein' framed-up for Mrs. Waring's murder."

But he tilted his head. "I might disagree with that assessment. No evidence has been planted that would implicate Grainston in Mrs. Waring's death."

She paused, seeing his point. "Oh—right. If this was a frame-up, it wasn't very well-done; the killer needed to plant a murder weapon, or a note, or somethin'."

"Yes. More likely this was an attempt to create a false trail, because the killer wants to obscure what the feather actually signifies."

Doyle raised her brows. "Do *you* know what the feather signifies?"

"I do not," he replied, and it was true.

She eyed his profile. "So; you think this murder is tryin' to throw us off the trail in the other feather murders—not that we've much of a trail to begin with—and so they've produced a peacock feather in a completely unrelated death."

"Yes; something like that."

Having run out of all patience, she ordered, "Spill, please; you're tryin' to stall, and it's makin' me very nervous."

In an even tone, he revealed, "I believe Sir Vikili is behind Grainston's death."

There was a moment of astonished silence as she stared at him, bereft of words. "Holy *Mother*, Michael; why—why would you think this?"

"Because I believe it was Javid who murdered Mrs. Waring."

He continued to watch the road ahead as she gaped at him, unable to help herself. "Mother a' *Mercy*, Michael—I'm goin' to fall out of the car. Why would *Javid* want to kill Tricia Waring?"

"I am not certain. But in light of the housekeeper's testimony, Javid is the only plausible suspect."

With acute dismay, Doyle assessed this pronouncement and found that she could not disagree—and shame on her; it only served to show what Acton had taught her when she was just a rookie detective—you follow the evidence, even when it leads you somewhere implausible. Doyle had let her preconceptions cloud her judgment, but she shouldn't have; after all, Javid had been involved in murky doings in the past, and—come to think of it—Sir Vikili had already shown he was willing to commit murder so as to protect her.

In wonder, Doyle shook her head. "It's so hard to believe, Michael—why *on earth* would she do such a thing?"

"I do not know. I imagine she is under some sort of compulsion, and it would explain the use of the feathers—she may be required to leave them as a warning to the other players."

Slowly, Doyle said, "So; you think she killed the CI, too."

"Almost certainly."

Thinking this over, Doyle concluded, "You think she's bein' blackmailed, or threatened."

"Yes. It only follows, since she was acting under threat when she was involved in the earlier iteration of this rig." He glanced at her. "She is very useful to them; due to the nature of her work, she has access to nearly everyone in the artworld. I imagine she acts as a go-between, even if she is no longer the person who is producing the fake artwork, and that this was her role when she painted Mrs. Waring's portrait. She was given access to kill the woman, and to leave a symbolic warning."

But Doyle frowned in confusion. "Wait—wait a blessed minute, Michael, that doesn't make much sense. If Javid's supposed to act as some sort of assassin, why was she botherin' to paint the woman's portrait?"

"It gave her access, and obscured her true motive," he pointed out. "She'd a valid reason to be on-site."

But slowly, Doyle shook her head. "I don't know, Michael—it seems so—so over-complicated, if that was the plan. Not to mention we still don't understand why the villains behind this rig would want Mrs. Waring dead, in the first place—they needed her famous name."

"Yes—I will admit that is the most puzzling aspect. It may be that Javid is being used as a pawn by another player—that there is indeed a turf-war involving this rig, and a rival underworld faction is seeking to disrupt the theatre's connection."

"I could see that," Doyle said thoughtfully. "Denisovich has been weakened—I think Sasha was his backbone, and whipped him up to do the awful things he did. But now she's dead, and mayhap another player has decided to move in—now that he's without her—and that other player is tryin' to cut him off at the knees."

"Perhaps. Of course, it could be simpler than that; Denisovich decided that Mrs. Waring was more of a liability than she was useful, and so he eliminated her. The same as the CI at the bakery—they were simply preemption-murders, and the feather is an attempt to obscure the true motive."

Doyle blew out a dismayed breath. "No matter the reason, Michael, it's so hard to believe that Javid would knuckle-under—especially after what she's been through at the hands of these awful people. Not to mention that now she's not so very helpless, with Sir Vikili in her corner." Doyle's scalp prickled, and she frowned. "Although she's pregnant; I wonder if that could explain it—she feels more vulnerable."

"Perhaps."

But Doyle was finding it hard to accept her own working-theory. "I don't know; you'd think her pregnancy would have the opposite effect—would steel her spine against these evildoers. And there's somethin' else that's important—let me think what it is."

Briefly, she shut her eyes, searching for the elusive thought. "Oh; recall that I'd the sense from the portrait that Javid didn't like Mrs. Waring, much. So that doesn't add up, if our workin'-theory is that Javid's a pawn to compulsion or blackmail."

"Perhaps you are mistaken," he offered gently. "By all accounts, there was little to dislike, when it came to Mrs. Waring."

Reluctantly, Doyle had to concede, "Right—everyone agrees that the woman was mild as milk, so it truly doesn't make a lot of sense that Javid would up and murder her, out of nowhere. Although you have to admit that the portrait-sittings allow Javid to get a good bead on people, and what makes them tick. Mayhap Mrs. Waring was a villain, too—despite all appearances—and Javid saw through her."

"It seems implausible that she'd inspire such a high level of animosity during a portrait sitting, though."

"Aye," Doyle reluctantly agreed. "And there's the CI, too—no portrait-sittin' there—and so I suppose we're back to compulsion or blackmail as the motive. And Sir Vikili is worried that you've figured out Javid is the murderess, and so he's dragged another corpse across your path so as to throw a wrench in."

"Yes. I imagine Javid has an ironclad alibi for Grainston's time-of-death."

She glanced over at him. "D'you think Sir Vikili knows you know this is a misdirection-murder?"

"Almost certainly. But with this murder, he has given his wife a reasonable-doubt defense, which he also knows I know."

Thoroughly frustrated, Doyle scolded, "Shame on the both of you; this is exactly what happens when you're all tied-up in the mutual skullduggery, husband; you didn't want to straight-out arrest Javid, and now an innocent man's been murdered because of it."

With gentle remonstrance, he reminded her, "I didn't have sufficient evidence to arrest Javid, Kathleen. I still don't."

She blew out a breath, and—with a mighty effort—reined in her temper. "Aye—you didn't. Sorry I'm snappin' at you, but you have to admit that everythin' would be miles easier if there weren't all these cross-considerations, makin' it harder to do our jobs."

"It is the nature of the beast, I'm afraid."

"Well, it shouldn't be half so complicated," she insisted. And since this was teetering on the edge of one of their discussions about how everyone was not as black-and-white as she thought it should be, she sidestepped that whole rigmarole and moved on to the million-pound question. "What are you goin' to do?"

He took a breath, his chest rising and falling. "I am not yet certain. Again, I'd suggest that you speak with the housekeeper a second time, and follow-up on whether anyone else was present when Javid went into the house."

The penny dropped, and Doyle said, "Because you're thinkin' it might be whoever's forcin' her to do this."

"That, and I'd like to be certain Javid was alone with the victim during the sittings." He glanced at her. "Be careful how you go about questioning the housekeeper."

Doyle nodded, since this much seemed obvious. Denisovich —if he was the one behind all this—wouldn't hesitate to kill Miss Senak, too, if he thought she'd make a likely witness for the prosecution.

Suddenly struck with a disturbing suspicion, she warned, "And don't you dare try to have Miss Senak take the fall for these murders, husband—the poor thing doesn't deserve it."

It went without saying that Acton would strive mightily to divert suspicion away from Javid—there was a long history of Acton and Sir Vikili doing favors for one another, and this would be the biggest favor of all—save for that time when Acton had charged-in like the cavalry to save the artist from being tossed into the vasty deep, of course; small wonder the woman was afraid of these people.

And it also went without saying that a DCI shouldn't be

casting about to help find a defense for a murderer, but here they were. Everyone's got divided loyalties, Doyle thought a bit crossly, including me; I can't very well grass-out my husband and have him thrown in the nick—I've got mouths to feed.

With a resigned acceptance of the shades of grey that were popping-up all around her like a jack o' the clock, she pleaded, "At least tell me, husband, that Williams is in Dublin to do a take-down and thus put an end to this miserable mess."

"We shall see," was his rather disappointing reply. "Mainly, Williams is hoping to shake a few trees in the hope that someone panics. It is a difficult case to prove."

She made a face. "Not to mention you think you're dealin' with a bent warrant-magistrate, whose palm is bein' greased."

"That, too. We need irrefutable evidence."

The words reminded her of the ghost's urgings, and so Doyle decided there was no time like the present to run the idea by Acton. "You know, Michael, if Rolph's in charge of the buildin'—and we know that our Rolph's the weakest of weak links—mayhap it would be useful for me to go over there and chat him up—all guileful and innocent-like. If I could get him to admit that there's artwork being funneled from the buildin' into the yachts, we'd have 'exigent circumstances' and you can side-step the crooked magistrate."

This, because the police did not need a search-warrant if they had first-hand knowledge of a crime, and were concerned that evidence might be destroyed in the time it would take to obtain a warrant.

Acton was silent, thinking this over, and so she added,

"Rolph's just the type to be boastful, and drop information that he shouldn't."

Slowly, her husband replied, "It is a good idea, but I am not certain that Rolph is cognizant of how this rig operates. In fact, I tend to think that he does not know."

Since Acton didn't have a ghost priming him, Doyle felt compelled to explain, "But that's the whole point, Michael. Rolph's a nodcock—and the last person anyone would trust with important information—but he's right there in the thick of it, managin' the buildin'. If he's in the dark about the rig, that will only make it easier to get him to implicate his uncle, all unknowin'—or at least, give us enough to claim exigent circumstances." Quoting the ghost, she added, "Rolph doesn't know what he knows."

She could see that this potential plan had caught his interest, and he replied, "Perhaps. Although any contact must appear as a happenstance."

"Say no more," she declared; "I can 'happenstance' with the best of 'em."

He smiled slightly. "It means something unplanned. A pleasure-outing, with no hint of official business. A fishing expedition with the children, perhaps."

"No," she declined firmly. "Fish are the work o' the devil."

"A boating expedition?" he mused. "There is an electric boat rental, on that very dock."

Doyle made a face. "That's only a peg down from your fishin' idea, husband—you know I'll be sick as a cat, if I get on a boat."

"The marina water should be smooth, though," he said. "The idea has merit, but it would have to be carefully handled."

"Say no more, husband; 'careful' is my middle name."

He smiled slightly. "I might disagree, and I have the grey hairs to prove it."

"They only make you look more distinguished," she declared. "Faith, you should be thankin' me."

CHAPTER 26

Since they were nearly back to headquarters, Acton asked, "You'd asked to meet at the bench; what did you wish to speak about?"

"Oh—I wanted to tell you about my Rolph-idea. And there was somethin' else that was bitin' at me; it seems a paltry thing, now—considerin' the Javid-angle—but I was wonderin' why Basil Waring married his wife. I think it's important, for some reason; it was an odd pairin', and the housekeeper said she never spoke of him after he died." Knitting her brow, Doyle added, "In fact, Miss Senak had the sense that Mrs. Waring was *ashamed*—that's the very word she used."

"Perhaps this is another subject you could raise with Miss Senak, then."

He doesn't think it's important, Doyle realized, and I suppose it isn't—the motivation for Waring's marrying his wife doesn't much matter, because none of this is a mystery—it all boils down to funding the money-laundering operation. In homicide cases, the motivator is almost always love or money, and in this one there's an obvious fortune at play. So instead of spouting more working-theories as to what motivated who to do what, I should put on my detective-hat and focus on rounding-up some irrefutable evidence from Rolph the weak-link.

You're wrong, her instinct informed her; love is indeed the motivator.

With some surprise, she considered this unlikely thought. Obviously, Javid wasn't murdering people out of love, so it didn't seem to make much sense. Denisovich? Mayhap he was murdering people in memory of his late wife? It certainly didn't seem so—Lanska was all about her political causes rather than money-making schemes, and there would be no reason for Denisovich to murder Mrs. Waring and the CI in her honor—not to mention that a lot of time had already passed since her death. So; who'd murdered these two victims out of love? It made no sense a'tall, and mayhap her trusty instinct had gone a bit haywire—sometimes it did.

Her husband's voice interrupted her thoughts. "I am wondering if perhaps I should look into purchasing the floor below us. We will need more room, after Mary is born."

Doyle smiled. Acton had been happily living his hermit-life in the fancy top floor of their fancy residential building until he'd married his unlikely bride, and with the advent of the two boys and the necessary servants—necessary because Acton was an aristocrat, and so of course servants were necessary—he'd purchased the floor below them so it could be devoted to bedrooms for children, security and the aforesaid servants. And now—apparently—he was feeling a bit crowded, yet again.

"You know, Michael, my mum and me lived very comfortably in one room with a sink and a stove." This, because Doyle had grown-up with a single mother who'd barely managed to make ends meet.

"Will we move the boys into the same bedroom, then?" This, said with some trepidation.

"Let's give it a try. We can only cross our fingers and hope they'll get some sleep. Tommy'd love it, and I think Edward wouldn't mind."

"Very well," he said, and took her hand. Unspoken was the understanding that Doyle had never been comfortable living in luxury with servants underfoot, and so she would naturally oppose any plans to create a London mansion to rival Trestles.

"Poor you," she teased. "You should have aimed for a wife who appreciated the finer things."

"I will confess that I was not aiming for a wife, at all."

"The joke's on you, then; God's havin' a good laugh."

"I cannot complain."

"Just goes to show. At least I'm somewhat useful when it comes to solvin' cases."

He ventured, "I don't suppose there's any chance you would consider stepping back, when Mary is born?"

She realized that this was the reason he'd brought-up the subject in the first place, and since this was familiar ground—they'd gone over it many a time—she replied in a mild tone, "We do good work together, Michael. And the part-time schedule does seem to be workin' out well."

"It is dangerous work," he observed, with the smallest hint of stubbornness.

But she only eyed him in amusement. "That's doin' it too brown, my friend; you've got me wrapped in cotton-wool—not that I don't appreciate it, of course, but there's no danger to be had between you, and Williams, and the security team. I can't even dash my foot on a stone."

"Something to consider, nonetheless."

"I will," she agreed, mainly to placate him. "Although if you're so concerned, you shouldn't be plottin' a boat-ride when little Mary's already makin' me green-about-the-gills."

"The idea is a good one," he admitted. "An outing with the children would afford an excellent excuse to go over there, with the hope of witnessing something incriminating."

"You can't come," Doyle warned. "You'd give the game away."

"No; but if you bring along the security-team it wouldn't be thought unusual. I think it would be well-worth the effort." He glanced at her. "Only make certain the boys wear life-vests."

"And me, too," she teased. Doyle—rather famously—couldn't swim.

"You, most of all," he added, and leaned over to kiss her.

CHAPTER 27

Once at work, Doyle decided she was willing to do almost anything to avoid looking at tedious CCTV tape—especially in this instance, where the wily Sir Vikili wasn't about to leave incriminating evidence behind—and so she rang up Tanya Senak, who answered the phone immediately. "Officer Doyle; have you caught the killer?"

"No arrests as yet," Doyle confessed, with a full measure of guilt. "But I'd like to meet, so as to give you an update. How about that coffee-place again?"

"Yes, I will be there."

A short time later, Doyle again greeted the young woman as they settled into a quiet table. Miss Senak looked a bit pulled-about—anxious to hear Doyle's report—and Doyle felt a twinge of pity; the young woman was determined to seek-out justice for her mistress, but now the odds were even more stacked against her, what with the illustrious

Chief Inspector running interference on behalf of the murderer.

More shades of grey, she thought with a mental grimace, and then firmly reminded herself that no one could truly count on justice this side of heaven. It was cold comfort, however, in light of the young woman's distress, and so she asked with some sympathy, "How are you doin', Miss Senak? If you're lookin' for another position, I've a friend who runs a bakery—she'd treat you kindly, if you don't mind risin' early."

The housekeeper's face immediately brightened. "Oh—oh, yes, I am looking for a new position—thank you; thank you so much, Officer Doyle."

"Are these the pearls Mrs. Waring gave you?" This, because the housekeeper was—rather incongruously—sporting a long double-strand of pearls, hanging between the lapels of her rather threadbare coat.

"Yes." Fingering them, the young woman bowed her head. "Mrs. Waring told me she was sorry she couldn't pay me more, and so she gave them to me—she said not to tell anyone, and no one would know."

"Well, that was kind of her," Doyle said, and then mentally girded her loins so as to do a bit of equivocating. "We're still lookin' into Mrs. Waring's death, but we're a bit puzzled because we can't find a motive for murder. The theatre-people may have been bullyin' her for money, but they'd no reason to kill her because she was readily givin' it to them and besides, they needed her to be the figurehead."

Listening intently, the girl asked, "The figurehead? Yes, what is this?"

"Her husband was famous, and people were more likely to donate their money because she was his widow," Doyle explained. "And so, they needed her alive."

"Oh," the witness said with a little frown. "I see."

"So; the murderer may not have been a theatre-person, but we've havin' trouble findin' out who went in and out of the house, since you weren't there on the day she died. I know we've already asked, but can you think carefully; did Mrs. Waring give anyone else the code—anyone a'tall?"

Slowly, the young woman shook her head. "Other than Mr. Grainston, no—and even then, I cannot be certain. I know of no others."

"Javid?" Doyle prompted.

"Oh—I do not think so," Miss Senak offered doubtfully. "She always rang the bell when she came—she was very courteous."

"Did anyone ever come in with Javid?" Doyle asked in a casual tone. "I don't know how it works—does she have an assistant who carries her brushes, and such?"

But the young woman shook her head. "No—she always came alone."

"Did anyone else visit Mrs. Waring around the times that Javid was there? Mayhap one of Mrs. Waring's friends, comin' by watch the sessions?"

Again, the witness shook her head. "Not that I know, Officer Doyle—although I was not always in the house for the sessions." She then added, "And Mrs. Waring had no friends."

"Save you," Doyle offered sincerely. "And she was lucky to have you."

"No—she was not lucky," the young woman observed sadly. "Poor lady."

Seeing an opening, Doyle ventured, "I think you mentioned that you felt she was ashamed, for some reason."

"Yes," the witness agreed in a low voice. "She was ashamed—ashamed that she wasn't strong enough to stand up to them. It grieved her."

But Doyle frowned, suddenly struck with the strangeness of this. "Are you sure? Mrs. Waring lived a very comfortable life, after all—especially considerin' where she'd come from. She was famous, and—from what I can tell—the theatre-people catered to her, tryin' to keep her happy. Faith, you'd think she'd fallen into a dream."

Doyle lifted her gaze to the windows for a moment, thinking about this. "Aye; and you'd also think she'd want to honor her husband by continuin' his legacy—he'd gifted her a life of ease, after all. Why would it grieve her, to give the theatre-people their fundin'? Did she want to leave London, and go home?"

"Oh, no—you do not understand." The housekeeper leaned forward, and explained earnestly, "It was the opposite; she was ashamed because she did not do as her husband asked. It was he who said don't give them the money, anymore."

Doyle blinked, since this disclosure seemed to make no sense a'tall. "Why would Basil Waring not want his theatre to get his money?"

But she was not to be enlightened, because Miss Senak slowly shook her head. "I don't know. I think—I think that is why he married her, because he trusted her to keep it from them. But then she did not do it, and she was ashamed."

Doyle gazed at the young woman with a touch of confusion, trying to process this latest wrinkle. So—mayhap Basil Waring had become aware that the theatre was involved in the artwork-rig, and had married his unlikely bride so that she'd stand firm against them, after he'd died? Tricia was a Midlands farmgirl, and presumably salt-of-the-earth; it would explain why he'd unexpectedly married her when he'd not been inclined to marry at all—by virtue of law, a wife would be in a strong position to protect his assets after his death.

Turning this idea over in her mind, Doyle lifted her gaze to the windows again. The only flaw in this plausible theory was the obvious question; why hadn't Basil Waring simply withheld the money, himself? If he'd unearthed the artwork rig—and was unhappy about it—then why wouldn't he have acted whilst he was alive? He was a powerful man, in his theatre-circles.

Doyle's scalp prickled and she shut her eyes, trying to catch the elusive thought. Unless—unless it wasn't the artwork-rig that he was worried about; unless he was concerned about something even more sinister. He'd died four years ago—unexpectedly? Doyle wasn't sure. And meanwhile, Sasha Lanska was haunting the fair Doyle's dreams—but she'd died at a later time, and it didn't seem connected—Lanska's death was at least a year after Basil Waring's, mayhap? Faith, she should act like a decent detective and put together a timeline, because there was something here—something that would explain why this sequence of events had gone down the way it had. Lanska's patron—and fellow Russian, lest we forget—hadn't wanted his money to support his theatre any longer, even though he'd apparently made this decision in secret, with none the wiser. He'd then gone to great lengths to make certain that the plan went forward—what with his unexpected marriage to someone he thought he could trust to follow his directives. Why? Of course, he'd always been a secretive fellow, apparently—his Russian heritage was kept secret; mayhap the fact that he hid his origins had something to do with it? But Denisovich was Russian, too—and made no bones about it—so why was Waring's heritage something that was shrouded in mystery? After all, Lanska hailed from his homeland, too—it wasn't like there weren't any fellow-Russians, thick on the ground. Faith, the theatre-folk and the media loved their radical Russians—it would have only added to Waring's mystique. So; why was it such a secret?

Suddenly, she stilled. Hold—hold a blessed minute; Basil Waring was a—what had Acton called it?—a White Russian, being as his family had opposed the Bolsheviks, way back when. So; yet again, tribal loyalty was rearing its head and small wonder he'd hidden his origins, since that wouldn't have flown well with his fellow theatre-people—let alone his leading actress.

So, he'd kept his heritage a secret, but it didn't seem to be much of a sticking-point for him, since he'd rubbed along with everyone his entire career, and avoided any political controversies. Faith, you need look no further than the fact that he'd worked cheek-by-jowl with Lanska to show that he hadn't felt strongly about such things. But then, for some reason, he'd abruptly married his unlikely wife and had quietly moved to put his fortune in her supposedly-trustworthy hands. Why? What was that timeline, again? About four years ago? Four years ago.

"Holy Mother of God," Doyle suddenly breathed, as the penny dropped.

Confused, Miss Senak asked, "Your pardon?"

"I'll let you know about the bakery job," Doyle said, as she abruptly rose to her feet. "But just now, I've got to go meet my husband at a bench."

CHAPTER 28

Acton had more than his share of irons in the fire, of course, but this time he agreed to come immediately, no doubt recognizing the urgency in his wife's voice. When Adrian dropped Doyle off at the park, Acton was already waiting at the pavement, and he paused a moment to have a quiet word with the driver.

He's asking him to stay close, Doyle decided; this park might be a good place for a private conversation, but it was also exposed to the public and—after all—Acton was turning up the heat on the villains; never too cautious, was our Acton.

Impatiently, she tugged on her husband's arm as they turned to walk toward their favorite bench. "Holy Mother, Michael; I went to speak with Miss Senak, and I think I've figured it all out."

"Excellent. Shall we sit?" he asked.

"I don't think I can," she confessed. "Wait 'till you hear this

—I was askin' her about why Mrs. Waring felt ashamed, and she said she thought it was because the woman wasn't doing what Basil wanted her to—she was *supposed* to be withholdin' the money from the theatre. That's why he married her, but she didn't uphold her end of the bargain, and kept knucklin' under."

With a knit brow, he considered this as they came to a halt before their bench. "He wasn't happy about the money-laundering, perhaps, and was afraid the theatre would sustain repercussions."

"That's what I thought at first, too—but then I thought; why wouldn't he just withhold the money himself, and tell them to knock it off? Why was it such a secret, that he went to such lengths? And then I thought about his other secret—how he didn't want anyone to know he was Russian, which seems a bit strange since Sasha Lanska was, and everyone loved her for it."

"His family were White Russians, Acton reminded her gently. "Perhaps not something that would have been appreciated, in the circles in which he ran."

"Exactly," she pronounced in triumph. "And he rubbed along with everyone—faith, even with his leadin' actress, who was on the other side of the fence—for years and years without any problem. Until suddenly, he up and marries Tricia and puts her in charge of his trust—did it in secret, like he didn't want anyone to know that the money was going to be tied-up after he was gone." She paused. "It happened around four years ago, Michael—think about what else happened, around four years ago."

She could see the light dawn in his eyes. "Ah. The fentanyl murder plot."

She nodded. "Aye; Lanska and her cohorts were hatchin' their plot to kill Gemma. He must have found out—found out his money was going to support such a despicable thing, and that was a bridge too far for him. He didn't want to confront them outright—mayhap he was nervous about what they'd do—so he did the next best thing, and tried to turn off their fundin' after he died. Only Tricia didn't uphold her end, and so it was all in vain."

There was a small pause, whilst her husband took her hand in his. "Well done," he said with all sincerity.

She grimaced slightly. "I feel as though it took me far too long—I was distracted by the peacock feather, but now even that makes perfect sense."

Her husband gazed at her for a moment, and then confessed, "I am lost, I'm afraid."

"The peacock feather shows Javid's motive for murder—and I'm not sayin' it's an excusable motive, but to her mind it's a good one. Nazy told me that the Persian people have a fable—they don't much like peacocks, because a peacock helped the serpent convince Eve to eat the apple. So, they think peacocks are damned, and that's why they screech so."

"I see," said Acton thoughtfully.

"The feather was a reproach, Michael. When Williams saw Waring's murder-scene, he said this must be a reproach-suicide because there's no such thing as a reproach-murder, but there he's wrong. Javid must have found out why Mrs. Waring was so unhappy during the portrait sittin'—faith, she probably found out about the plot against Gemma, too—and it triggered her; Mrs. Waring was an aider-and-abettor to evil, and Javid's not havin' it—not after what she's been through."

Doyle frowned, thinking about this. "Javid's had her own glimpse into hell, and I imagine that changes a person—not that it's an excuse for murder, of course, but at least it makes some sense. She's sick to the back teeth of weak people who won't step-up to stop evil, because she was just such a weak person, herself, once upon a time—and she almost paid a terrible price for her weakness. And then she hears about this wicked plot against a child—just as she's goin' to have a child herself. She must have been that triggered."

Acton nodded. "And we can presume she must have discovered—perhaps from Sir Vikili—that the CI at the bakery was playing both sides."

Doyle stared at him. "Aye—I forgot about the CI, but I suppose you could say that both her victims were takin' blood-money to look the other way, and Javid wasn't havin' it." Doyle repeated, "It all adds up—the feather was a reproach to those who were aiding-and-abetting evil."

But Acton tilted his head in mild disagreement. "I believe the feather was more along the lines of a message."

Doyle blinked. "A message? To who?"

"To Javid's husband, who would also understand its significance."

She stared at him for a long moment. "Mother a' Mercy; you're right—she's married to the greatest aider-and-abettor of them all. And now she's pregnant, and she's goin' scorched-earth because she wants him to mend his ways." Doyle blew out an astonished breath. "Who would have guessed it? She's made of steel, down to her toes."

The words hung in the air for a moment, and Doyle was

suddenly aware of the parallel to their own marriage—save that Doyle's reproaches never seemed to make much of an impact. Of course, Acton had his demons, and so she had to step carefully—it wasn't quite the same situation.

Shying away from this uncomfortable thought, Doyle asked a bit briskly. "So, now what?"

"I will have a word."

Doubtfully, Doyle ventured, "Will that help? The man's in a cleft-stick—he can't betray his clients."

"No, I will have a word with Javid."

The light dawned, and Doyle could see the wisdom in this. "You saved her life; we can hope that she'll listen to you."

"Yes. And in the end, she won't want this exposed. It is a private matter between herself and her husband."

Annoyed, Doyle chided, "Murder shouldn't be a 'private matter', Michael."

"In this case, I'm afraid it is," he pointed out. "It would be impossible to prove."

"Aye," Doyle reluctantly agreed. "Not to mention that she'd have a mighty fine defense lawyer, all up in your grill."

CHAPTER 29

"I must make things right," Lanska insisted, her voice rich and resonating in the cold darkness. "*The wheel is come full circle.*"

Doyle made a face. "Speakin' of bein' made of steel down to your toes."

"*Fair is foul, and foul is fair,*" the actress admitted. "I know you don't want to believe me, but you must."

"More like I don't understand ruthless women who don't care about anythin' save for themselves," Doyle retorted. "You and Lisa Davies both fit that category; she used to sneer at me like she sneered at Javid—although she had to be careful, else Acton would bring the hammer down." She paused, considering this, then admitted, "Acton tends to overreact, when it comes to me."

"Yes; a solicitous husband," the ghost agreed. "There are more than a few, in this tale."

But Doyle didn't much like this implied comparison. "At

least I try to use my influence over my husband for good—not like you. I'm tryin' to be an Esther—steerin' Acton away from his bloodthirsty ways—but you're more along the lines of a Jezebel—leadin' your husband into sin. And shame on him, for followin' you."

"My death devastated him," the ghost remarked. "Which is only to be expected, for such a devoted husband."

This seemed a strange sort of thing to say, and Doyle frowned. "Then mayhap you should have considered his feelings when you were hatchin' your evil plots."

"Oh, I am; believe me, I am," the ghost said, and smiled slightly.

Warily, Doyle regarded her companion; she'd the feeling that Lanska was having a bit of a joke at her expense—laughing at her, behind her actress-mask.. "I doubt it; that's the problem with women like you—equal parts selfish and ruthless. We see them a lot, in this business; they never give a thought to anyone else—do whatever they wish and don't give two pins about the wreckage they leave in their wake."

At this home-truth, the self-satisfied smile disappeared, to be replaced by an earnest expression. "Please—you wrong me; I am consumed with making this right." She then lifted her hands to hold them before her face. "*Will all great Neptune's ocean wash this blood clean from my hand? No, this my hand will rather the multitudinous seas incarnadine, making the green one red.*"

After holding the pose for a beat, the ghost lowered her hands and sighed. "Oh, how I miss the stage. There is nothing like it."

"Then you should have stuck with what you were good at,"

Doyle offered without sympathy. "But instead here you are, and havin' to repent fastin'."

"You are unkind," the ghost said with quiet sadness. "I was hoping that you would understand."

"Not a chance," Doyle declared stoutly. "For starters, I'm not one to murder people, for love or money."

"I was murdered out of love," the ghost noted.

A bit taken aback, Doyle acknowledged the truth of this. "Aye—I suppose you were. You went after Savoie's family, and that's not the smart play; he's not one to take such a thing lyin' down."

"Yes. If only I'd known."

Doyle felt compelled to point out, "You shouldn't have been plottin' to murder children to begin with, no matter whose they are."

"It is a terrible failing," the ghost admitted.

There was a small silence, and once again Doyle entertained the uneasy feeling that—despite the ghost's earnest expression—she was baiting the fair Doyle; the actress was having a private joke at her expense. "Don't you snark at me," Doyle warned; "that won't wash."

"Help me," the ghost beseeched, once again the picture of humble remorse. "Help me to right all wrongs."

CHAPTER 30

The next morning, Doyle thought over her latest ghostly encounter as she helped the boys get ready for the day. She'd the sure sense that the ghost was mocking her a bit—making snide references that Doyle didn't quite catch, being as the fair Doyle wasn't always quick on the uptake when it came to snide references. So, caution was advised; it was possible that this little morality-play about "making things right" was all an act—the woman was a great actress, after all.

On the other hand, the ghost had been telling the truth when she'd said—again and again—that such was her intent. And she'd also acknowledged that Savoie had murdered her out of love—rather a strange take, but it showed she wasn't so hardened that she couldn't see the justice of it.

The main thing, of course, was that it did seem as though she was trying to steer them toward some rock-solid evidence, even if it turned out to be at her own son's expense. Mayhap she was truly repentant, after all—or mayhap she was trying to give Rolph a fright, so as to steer him onto a better path. He'd likely not suffer overmuch, since Sir Vikili would no doubt stand as his counsel and work his usual magic. Unless Javid managed to turn that trick, of course, and convince her husband to change his clientele from the wicked oppressing to the poor and oppressed—talk about a leopard changing his spots, that would take the palm. But it was possible, of course; only see how Acton had changed his own spots—and Savoie, too. The ghost was right; solicitous husbands were thick on the ground, in this tale.

Her scalp prickled as she buttoned Edward's coat, and she wondered why it would. Denisovich may have doted on Lanska, but the ghost hadn't loved her husband in return—Doyle would bet her teeth; the actress was incapable of loving anyone save herself. Still and all, there was no denying that she was telling the truth when she kept saying that she wanted to make things right, and Acton seemed to think the "happenstance" idea had merit—to go at this thorny case from the blabbing-Rolph angle, and thus circumvent the crooked magistrate.

I'll be extra cautious, Doyle decided as she gave her son a quick kiss; I don't trust this ghost a miser's mite, and so I'll be on the lookout for the slightest hint of ghostly double-dealing.

Therefore, she informed Reynolds on the walk to school, "I've decided to go ahead with a visit to the City Quay—d'you know those little boats you can rent out at the marina—the electric ones? That's what I think we'll do—it would be a fun outin' for the boyos."

The butler nodded. "Very good, madam. And I believe there

is a children's museum in the new development. Shall I investigate?"

Since any sort of museum would not be Doyle's cup of tea, she demurred, "I'm more interested in takin' a boat-ride, I think. The boys won't hold together for very long, anyways."

"Very true. When would you like to go, madam?"

Since Acton had wanted to make the attempt as soon as possible, she suggested, "Tomorrow, I think."

"Very good, madam; I will make the arrangements."

She cautioned, "Acton will want both Trenton and Adrian to come, since he won't be comin'."

"I will arrange for it, madam."

"And if you would, please contact Rolph Denisovich, just so he knows we'll be there for a visit. I should be civil and say hallo—I feel a bit badly that Acton served him such a trick at our wretched dinner-party."

In a neutral tone, Reynolds replied, "I am not certain the young man will appreciate your olive branch, madam."

Shrewdly, Doyle disagreed. "He won't be able to resist the chance to show-off—he's that sort."

"A fair point."

"Good, then—it's all settled."

With a sense of accomplishment, Doyle congratulated herself on the plan's coming together—she could be as canny as Acton, when she put her mind to it. Well, mayhap that was a boast too far—since no one was as canny as Acton—but every once in a while she came close, even if it was only at the prompting of questionable ghosts.

And—thinking along these lines—Doyle decided to accomplish yet another task as she rang-up Mary Savoie. "Mary, I've a favor to ask, if you won't mind."

"Of course, Lady Acton."

"I've a witness in a case whose employer was killed. She seems a good sort—loyal, and such. She needs a new job, and I'm wonderin' if she could help out at the bakery—at least for the time bein'.

"Oh—this is a happy coincidence; we've actually been thinking of hiring a nanny. I've been bringing Hannah into the bakery, but now she's getting old enough to get into trouble, and so I need someone to watch her in the mornings. Philippe's been resisting, because he's wary about going through the agencies."

This, no doubt because the House of Acton had a spotty history when it came to the hiring of agency-nannies, but now they were fortunate to have Miss Cherry, which in turn reminded Doyle that Miss Cherry had a beau and it wouldn't be a surprise if the woman shortly retired from the nannying lists. Mayhap the fair Doyle should be the one looking to hire Miss Senak, instead.

Mary's voice broke into these rather dismaying thoughts. "I would like to see how she does with the children; could you give me her contact? I could arrange for a play date."

Suddenly struck, Doyle offered, "If you'd like, Mary, we're arrangin' for an outin' on one of those electric boats at the marina. You could bring the children along, and we could all meet up with Miss Senak—a bit less pressure on everyone."

"Oh—that sounds like a wonderful plan."

"Reynolds is gettin' it all arranged; he'll give you the details."

"Perfect—thank you so much."

Doyle warned, "Once you meet her, though, feel free to say 'no' if you don't think it would work out." This, because Mary was the sort of person who wouldn't dream of saying no, and there'd been times when her kind nature had landed her in the soup.

With a touch of humor in her voice, Mary replied, "I have to pay it forward, Lady Acton; I was a witness in want of a job too, once upon a time."

Doyle laughed. "Indeed, you were. See you soon."

Still smiling to herself, Doyle rang off. Mary's life had changed dramatically since that long-ago time when she'd been living in the projects, and it was something that the two of them shared in common; they'd gone from rags to riches because a man had fallen in love with them—a true-to-life fairy-tale. Of course, their fairy-tales had involved some harrowing episodes, but who would have known when Doyle had gone to interview Mary that their lives would become so intertwined? The young woman had been through a lot, since then—had tragically lost two husbands, poor thing—but now she seemed very content, running the bakery and married to—of all people—Philippe Savoie, which no one could have seen coming and just went to show you that love was a force unto itself, and was very much amused by anyone's attempts to control it.

She turned to Reynolds. "D'you hear that, Reynolds? Mary's comin' too, along with her children and the potential nanny. Make sure the boat's big enough."

"I believe they hold a dozen or so, madam. And if I may say

so, it is very kind of you to assist this young woman, who has need of employment."

"*The wheel is come full circle*," Doyle replied, with an air of wisdom.

CHAPTER 31

"I feel much better," Doyle reported to her husband. "You probably should have shaved, though."

"Sorry—should I get up?"

"No—don't move."

They were lying on the floor of their expansive shower, because Doyle had discovered that the cure for morning sickness was to lie on her back upon the warmth of the tiles with her husband's weight resting atop her. Before Edward was born, they'd practiced this cure in the main room, but due to the various persons who now inhabited the premises—including children who tended to climb out of their beds—they were relegated to the shower, which was actually rather enjoyable in that it was steamy and warm, and Doyle liked the way their voices echoed off the walls.

"I don't know as we can do this indefinitely."

"Hush, you; you're doin' fine."

She pronounced it "foine" so as to tease him, and then shifted, slightly—his prickly beard would leave a rash, but she wasn't about to budge; another benefit of the cure was that her husband was not someone who could lie atop his wife for very long without feeling amorous, and it was past time that he felt amorous. Her libido was hit-or-miss in early pregnancy, and so he tended to leave her alone, the knocker.

"Reynolds has contacted Rolph, and the plan's in train," she informed him.

"Must we speak of Rolph, just now?"

She giggled. "He's not your favorite, I think."

"Decidedly not."

"Well, he must do a decent job with the property management; Denisovich wouldn't risk it, otherwise."

"I thought we weren't going to speak of Rolph?"

"Callie, then," she teased. Callie was far from Acton's favorite, too.

"Perhaps we shouldn't speak at all," he suggested into her neck.

"Faith, husband; who d'you think you're married to? I'll be gabblin' 'til the day I die. How are things goin' with the Callie-Gabriel pairin'?"

"I am not certain," he admitted.

"Me, neither; she seemed a bit smitten with Seamus Riordan, if you ask me."

"Really?" he asked in surprise.

"Aye—not sure why he'd appeal—mayhap she has hidden depths."

"Doubtful," he replied.

"Love is the great redeemer," she advised. "I was just thinkin' about that, today."

He kissed her neck. "Always a revelation, to hear what you think about."

She laughed. "It's just as well that you keep what you think about well-hidden; it's probably dark and spidery."

"I think about you," he replied, and began nuzzling her neck.

This was a good sign, and so she tilted her head so as to grant him greater access. "You also think about Trestles, and smitin' your enemies."

"Not as much as I think about you, though."

"Is that so? I'm well-and-truly flattered; you've a bushelful of enemies to smite."

Reminded, he paused to caution, "Be careful what you say to Rolph—you'll be doing recon, only."

"Oh, I'm always in the mood for a bit of recon," she teased, moving her hand southward between them.

He made a soft sound in his throat, but made no attempt to put a halt to her ministrations, which was another good sign.

He cautioned, "If you see anything worthwhile, report to me. Under no circumstances are you to take matters into your own hands."

"Like this?" she teased, suiting word to action.

"Kathleen—"

She soothed, "No worries, Michael; I'll be subtle as a serpent and twice as guileful—it's what I'm known for."

He chuckled and she joined in with him, since the way his chest reverberated against hers was oh, so very pleasant and he was definitely responding to her touch.

"Try not to land the both of us before Professional Standards." This, because police had to be careful not to be accused of entrapment.

She scoffed, "As though Professional Standards wouldn't bow down and offer to shine your shoes, Michael. Doin' it too brown."

"Nevertheless, we should not do anything that might jeopardize the case; let's not grant Sir Vikili any boons."

"No boons a'tall, I promise. Not a single boon to be seen."

"You may wish to—"

"No more work-talk," she interrupted. "I'm tryin' to seduce you, here; don't make me have to pull-on my spikey black boots—the steam would probably ruin them."

"I suppose I've little choice," he murmured into her throat. "I am out-manned and out-gunned."

"Your gun is never out-manned," she teased wickedly, but then he silenced her mouth with his own.

CHAPTER 32

The following day, Doyle had decided that she should meet-up with Miss Senak before Mary's party arrived so that the young woman could be briefed about the nanny position. They now stood at a small distance from the electric-boat kiosk, where Adrian and Trenton had taken the boys to be fitted for their life-vests.

Miss Senak seemed nervous, and was a bit too dressed-up for the occasion, wearing a skirt and blouse. Around her neck she again wore the long double-strand of pearls—completely inappropriate, but Doyle decided that the young woman seemed to take comfort in them, and no one could fault her for it—what with Mrs. Waring's murder, her life had been turned upside-down.

"Mary's got three children," Doyle explained. "Emile who's eight, Gemma, who's six—almost seven, now, and Hannah, who's a toddler." Doyle debated whether to wade into the quagmire that was each child's parentage, but decided she'd leave that call to Mary. She also decided not to mention that she wouldn't be in the least surprised if there was soon to be a new baby—faith, this potential nanny-job was something of a daunting position when all was said and done, and this was without even touching on the fact that the father of the house was a notorious underworld kingpin.

"Have you any experience with children?" Doyle ventured.

The young woman offered, "I did babysit my cousins."

"Good enough," Doyle decided. "Mary's a gentle soul, so you'll have no problems on that front."

They were interrupted when they were hailed by Rolph Denisovich, who strode down the dock-ramp toward them, just as self-important and smarmy as Doyle remembered him to be. Although to be fair, the last time she'd seen him he was being escorted away for drunk-and-disorderly, so to see him swaggering down the dock and presumably sober was somewhat of an improvement.

"Ho, Rolph," Doyle called in a friendly fashion, to show that bygones were bygones. "Good to see you again."

If she'd anticipated the slightest hint of embarrassment, she was to be disappointed as Rolph airily remarked, "Where's that famous husband of yours? I could get him to invest in my building, and spread some of his money my way."

Doyle decided to ignore this sally, and instead gestured toward Miss Senak. "Here's Tanya Senak; she's come to join us for the boat ride."

"You're dressed for it; nice pearls," the young man joked.

But the derision behind the remark went unnoticed, as Miss

Senak blushed and replied with all sincerity, "Thank you. I was told they once belonged to a king."

Rolph smiled a bit patronizingly. "Were you? Some people will believe anything. Where're you from? You sound fresh off the boat."

Again, the girl blushed as she replied, "I am from Volyn."

"Are you?" Rolph said with a laugh. "I won't tell you where my family's from then, or you'll push me in the water."

"I would not," Senak protested with a shy smile—she was rather pretty, when she smiled—and it occurred to Doyle that she'd best make sure the naïve girl didn't fall victim to Rolph; they were lucky enough to have extracted Callie, back when she was under his sway. Unfortunately, he was handsome and glib, which seemed a fatal combination to many a fair damsel.

Firmly, Doyle interrupted to do a bit of probing, since there was evidence to be gathered—at least, according to the man's ghost-mother. "How are things goin', Rolph? This seems a nice-lookin' development."

With a self-satisfied air, the young man cast his gaze over the imposing building; sleek and many stories high so as to take advantage of the river-view. "Yes, another building in the inventory—this one should be quite the money-maker." In an offhand manner, he said to Miss Senak, "Perhaps you'd like a tour?"

"Thank you, but I must meet one of Officer Doyle's friends, and her children." Her color rising, the young woman disclosed, "I am interviewing to be a nanny."

With a small smirk, he eyed her. "Are you? Can't abide children, myself."

"Oh," Miss Senak said doubtfully. "I see."

"Although—we're opening a children's discovery museum," Rolph was quick to point out. "Up there—see? Over where that balcony is. It will be a money-maker for sure; pulls-in all the adults to spend in the shops, while the kiddos are running around the museum. There'll be a restaurant up there, too—very posh, so a high profit-margin."

"Oh," Senak admired, her eyes wide. "You must be a very good businessman."

"It's my uncle, really," Rolph confessed. "But I'm learning the ropes, since I'll have to take over for him, someday."

"Is the restaurant openin' soon?" Doyle asked innocently. A posh restaurant would be an excellent excuse to rotate art-work through, since such an expense could be written-off and there would be a plausible excuse to have it on the walls.

A trace of frustration entered the young man's voice. "Oh—well, the restaurant's been delayed—a lot of permitting required for a restaurant; you've no idea. The discovery museum is almost ready to go, though. Maybe your kiddos would like to come up to see it after their boat ride—we could do a test-run."

Doyle didn't hesitate to seize upon this golden opportunity to do a bit of nosing-about. "Why, that sounds wonderful, Rolph. And so kind of you."

"Yes," Miss Senak said with her shy smile. "You are so kind."

"Not at all," he demurred, his chest expanding.

"Mr. Denisovich—a word, please?"

At the interruption, Doyle looked up to see Mr. Elliott, the City Development authority who Acton suspicioned was on the take. The man was striding toward them, and not bothering to hide his extreme agitation. He's recognized me, Doyle concluded, and—the same as at the memorial service—he's not the sort of crook who can hide his alarm, when he's confronted with Scotland Yard's finest.

Which, of course, seemed to prove that Acton's theory was correct, and the Public Accounts scandal had at least one corrupt remnant in the City Development sector. And it was also clear that Mr. Elliott was a smarmy bureaucrat—unlike his Russian counterparts—and therefore he was not savvy enough to stay calm and bluff his way through this latest alarm. Faith, it was enough to make you feel sorry for the Russian-mafia types, who'd been compelled to enlist the man in their scheme.

Although mayhap they weren't going to tolerate him for very long—regardless of his usefulness—because yet again, Doyle was given the uneasy impression that the annoying Mr. Elliott wasn't long for this world. A preemption-murder, mayhap; he seemed far too wobbly for a co-conspirator, and so it was possible that his puppet-masters had decided he was too much of a liability.

Nothing she could do about it, of course—the man would think she was barking mad if she started issuing dire warnings—not to mention Acton would be most unhappy with her, if she went about trying to warn people that they were marked for death.

And so, Doyle did her best to convey the impression she'd nothing better to do than keep watch over her children as she carefully ignored the fact that Mr. Elliott was conferring in intense tones with Rolph, who wasn't bothering to hide his disdain.

CHAPTER 33

Mr. Elliott having been thoroughly rebuffed by Rolph—you could tell by his posture that he was very unhappy—the development official was left with little choice but to retreat back up the dock's ramp. To add insult to injury, he was forced to squeeze against the railing as Mary descended the ramp with her children, holding little Hannah on her hip as Gemma and Emile raced down at full speed, which was only to be expected of children who'd been confronted with a ramp.

"Stay close—no running," Mary cautioned the older children, even though it was too little and too late.

Doyle laughed. "A faint hope, to think that one or more won't wind-up with a wettin', Mary. Here's Tanya Senak—and you remember Rolph."

No doubt she did, since Mary had been present for the aforementioned drunk-and-disorderly incident, but she offered-up a friendly smile and greeted the young man with all good will. “You must come by and see how the bakery does, Rolph. We’ve remodeled the kitchen, and it looks quite different.”

“Not likely,” Rolph declared. He then explained to Miss Senak with a trace of condescension, “One of my first jobs was at the bakery—my uncle used to own the place. I’ve come a long way since then—now I manage his five-star properties.”

“Oh,” said Miss Senak, who then confessed, “I would prefer the bakery, I think.”

“It definitely smelt better,” he conceded, and Miss Senak laughed as though he’d said something very clever.

Best separate these two, thought Doyle with a twinge of alarm. “We should load up, but your children will need their life-vests first, Mary.”

As Mary’s children were kitted-out, Mary chatted in a friendly manner with Miss Senak whilst Rolph hovered rather awkwardly—trust him to not take his cue, and leave them to their outing. “We’ll be back in an hour or so,” Doyle hinted to him. To Mary, she advised, “Rolph has kindly offered to allow the children to visit the discovery museum before it officially opens.”

“Why, that’s wonderful, Rolph, I’m sure they will enjoy it.”

“Not at all; happy to give it a test-run, so to speak.” This, said a bit loudly in Miss Senak’s direction but she didn’t hear this show of generosity since she was chatting with Mary’s two older children.

The dock-workers then began the noisy process of getting the excited children loaded into the boat, with Adrian maintaining an unrelenting grip on little Tommy, who was never quite convinced that he couldn’t do whatever the older boys did.

Just as Doyle was mentally girding her loins to step aboard, she heard her name called-out and looked up in surprise to see Callie hurrying down the ramp, accompanied by Seamus Riordan, who was holding his hat on his head against the breeze. Cheerfully, the girl waved and called out, "Wait for us, please."

"Hallo, Callie, Mr. Riordan—here's a surprise."

Breathlessly, Callie informed her, "I hope you don't mind; Adrian mentioned the outing and I thought Seamus might enjoy it—it's such a touristy thing to do."

"You're both welcome, of course, although the children will probably drive you mad."

"Hallo, Rolph," Callie greeted her former beau. "Good to see you again."

Oh—now, this is a bit awkward, Doyle realized, and braced for Rolph to say something snarky and unpleasant.

But they were to be spared any spite, as the young man only offered a polite smile. "Good to see you, too." To Miss Senak, he explained, "We used to date, once upon a time."

"Come on," said Callie, laughing as she tugged on Seamus' arm. "Let's get in."

Doyle watched their interaction and thought; she's indeed smitten, and here's an unexpected turn of events. Small wonder Adrian seems a bit glum—not to mention that Gabriel doesn't need any more disappointments, poor man. Although we're lucky that Rolph doesn't seem at all dismayed—thank all available saints and holy angels; no one can make a scene quite like Rolph.

And speaking of such, as the newcomers squeezed into the boat Rolph idly leaned in to ask Doyle, "He doesn't seem her type; how'd she meet him?"

Oh-oh, Doyle suddenly realized; Mother a' Mercy but this is a rare bramble—if everything plays out as hoped, our Seamus, here, is going to put Rolph's father behind bars.

Fervently hoping that Acton was right, and that Rolph was not acquainted with the details of the money-laundering rig, Doyle replied in a breezy manner, "Oh—she met him at university; apparently, he's in town to get a degree on ancient manuscripts, or some such. Well-over my head, in any event."

"Huh," Rolph said, in a manner that managed to convey his skepticism that anything of interest could possibly happen at a university.

"If you'd come aboard, ma'am," the dock-worker called out to her.

"We'll be off," Doyle said to Rolph with some relief. "See you later."

The young man nodded. "I'll keep a watch-out for when you return."

Doyle couldn't help but notice that his gaze lingered on Miss Senak, even though her back was to him as she chatted with Mary, and decided it was a good thing that the young woman was going to work for Savoie's household—Savoie would nip any Rolph-overtures in the bud and probably cuff his ear, to boot.

Doyle decided she should settle next to Callie, and took the opportunity to remind the girl in a low tone, "I know you're doin' a kindness for Mr. Riordan, Callie, but you've got to be careful; he's an important witness and there are some very bad actors involved." No need to mention that they'd left some of the aforementioned bad actors behind them on the dock—it was something of a dilemma, because Doyle couldn't very well disclose any specifics about the Denisovich-doings to Callie, therefore any warnings were necessarily rather generalized.

"Oh, I know," the girl replied. "But I thought this wasn't very public, and the poor man deserves an outing—it's such a beautiful day."

But Rirodan's presence could be a problem for this particular recon mission, and so Doyle texted Acton, "Underway. R will give us a tour of premises. C here, she brought S, need direction."

But Acton didn't seem over-alarmed by this development, and replied, "D?"

He was referring to Denisovich, and Doyle replied, "No."

"Let me know."

"Right."

As she sheathed her mobile, Doyle belatedly realized she should probably have told him that Elliott had seen her, and stewin' like a barleycorn about it. I'll fill him in next text, she decided—I have to be careful not to look as though I'm reporting-in.

With this in mind, she relaxed a bit, happy to note that the water was indeed smooth, and that her recon mission was going exactly as hoped.

CHAPTER 34

There was little opportunity for conversation for the first few minutes, what with the children chattering in excitement and Adrian keeping a firm grip on Tommy, who was leaning over the side of the boat and watching, fascinated, as the water slid past the hull. But once they were comfortably underway, Doyle had a chance to ask Mary, "How's the house-huntin' goin'?" The Savoies were looking to move to a larger house on the outskirts of town.

"We've looked at a few properties," Mary replied. Leaning in, she confided, "I am so happy you mentioned Miss Senak; we're expecting."

Unsurprised, Doyle smiled. "Faith, Mary—that's wonderful."

Mary nodded. "It's early days, yet, so we haven't told the children."

"I'll not say, then. Me too, by the way; we'll both be havin' another round of babies to keep us on our toes—no rest for the weary."

Delighted, Mary exclaimed, "Isn't it lovely? I hope they'll be friends—it's such a blessing that our older ones are close."

You've no idea, thought Doyle, but aloud she said, "A'course they'll be friends, Mary; knowin' someone who owns a bakery is the next best thing to knowin' someone who owns a candy-store."

Mary laughed again, and Doyle felt compelled to remark, "And if anyone had told me when I first met Philippe Savoie that he was slated to be wearin' an apron in a charity bakeshop, I'd have thought they were barkin' mad and should be shriven besides."

With a rueful smile of acknowledgement, Mary defended, "He's a good soul, beneath it all."

Since Doyle already knew this—despite the Frenchman's rather hardened appearance—she readily agreed. "No arguments, here."

Another redemption love-story—where a woman turned out to be a good influence on what was once a bad man, she thought. Sasha Lanska was right—doting husbands were thick on the ground, in this tale. Here's hoping that she's also right about Rolph's having loose lips, and giving away his father's game.

Idly, Mary knit her brow. "How did you first meet Philippe, Lady Acton? He's a bit mysterious about it."

This, because Doyle had met Savoie whilst she was in the process of being assaulted under best-be-forgot circumstances. Blandly, she offered, "I was volunteerin' at the charity medical clinic, and we struck-up a conversation." Not the only thing that wound-up being struck, but no need to tell Mary chapter-and-verse.

Gemma called for Mary's attention, and Doyle felt herself relax a bit as she watched the children screech upon sighting a dead fish—screeching for the sake of screeching, as children were wont to do. All was going well, and she was cautiously optimistic; Lanska had urged her to come on-site and speak with Rolph, and it did seem that she was to be given a prime opportunity to nose-out some much-needed evidence. And—as an added bonus—because they'd been invited on the premises, there'd be no need to obtain a search-warrant if she saw anything suspicious firsthand—there was no longer the need to rely on exigent circumstances.

Of course, there was the rather unexpected development that Rolph appeared to be smitten with Miss Senak, but it seemed unlikely that this was an intended result of the ghost's maneuverings; the young man's mother wouldn't be remotely interested in matchmaking, since she hadn't a maternal bone in her body—not to mention any romance was thoroughly doomed, since things were about to get very dicey for the Denisovich family.

Despite all these promising developments, however, Doyle continued to entertain the niggling sense that she should remain wary; this particular ghost had been ruthless and conniving in life, and Doyle didn't have the impression that she was within hailing distance of the road to repentance.

Hard on this thought, Seamus Riordan rose to indicate he wanted to squeeze-in on her other side, and Doyle moved over to greet him with a smile. "How d'you like London, Mr. Riordan?"

The young man confessed, "I like the university, but the city is a bit too crowded for my taste." He paused. "I'm surprised you find it tolerable."

Doyle conceded, "Well, it's not Ireland, but you have to admit that Dublin's a bit over-crowded, too."

The young man nodded, but Doyle could see that he was worried about something, and was trying to decide what to say. Since he was an important witness in an important case, she asked with some concern, "Everythin' all right, then?"

To her surprise, he responded in Gaelic. "I wanted to ask you about the dog."

Doyle blinked, but replied in the same language. "You've a dog?"

"No—no." He paused. "There was a dog on the docks. I was wondering if it was a—a portent."

Utterly bewildered, she stared at him—remembering that the ghost had advised her to disregard any and all dog-portents. "I—I've no idea what you mean, I'm afraid. I didn't notice a dog—and I doubt they'd allow a dog on the dock in the first place."

"I don't think anyone else can see him, save you and me." He then met her eyes with some significance.

Doyle stared at him for a long, stunned moment. *Holy Mother of God*, she thought, as she felt herself blush to the roots of her hair. *Holy Mother of God.*

He continued earnestly, "I don't want to upset you, but it worries me."

"I don't know what you're talkin' about," she managed though stiff lips.

He ducked his head, and examined his hands. "I understand. I just wish I knew who he belonged to, and what he does here."

"What are you two saying?" Callie teased. "It's not fair."

"Nothin', Callie," Doyle managed. "Just testin' out my rusty tongue."

"I think it's important," Seamus repeated in a low tone.

Doyle pressed her lips together—what to do, what to do? After wrestling with it for a moment, she decided to reassure him in an oblique way, without necessarily confessing anything. "Gemma's stepfather had a dog—Raven, was his name." She paused. "He was very protective of her."

The young man raised his brows. "Raven? The last Tsar of Russia had a dog named Raven."

"I canno' talk to you," Doyle blurted out, in a sudden panic. "And do not, under any circumstances, say anythin' to my husband." Acton had already shown how he handled people who'd shown an interest in Doyle's uncanny abilities, and this fellow would be given short shrift, since such a thing was miles more important to her husband than any paltry Russian-mafia take-down. Holy Mother, what a mess.

"*Ceart go leor*; I'm sorry I upset you."

"Hush," she cautioned, and quickly moved away from him.

CHAPTER 35

Doyle was still trying to come to grips with Riordan's revelation when the boat ride came to an end, and a dock-worker leapt on the boat so as to bring it in. What to do? She decided to say nothing to anyone—especially Acton—and pretend it never happened. She'd never met another person with her perceptive abilities—or at least, not knowingly—and it had shaken her off her pins, a bit. Her instinct was to shun him, which—on second thought—seemed a bit drastic, since the two of them were strangers in a strange land. But nonetheless, she'd an overwhelming urge to put as much distance between them as possible—not to mention she was annoyed at him for having rattled her—faith, she'd never have said a thing to him, if the situation were reversed. Although to be fair, he may never have said anything save for the portent-dog that Lanska had told her to ignore. Interesting, that the fair Doyle hadn't caught sight of the dog this time around—in the past she'd seen him on occasion, quietly shadowing little Gemma.

"You're a bit pale, Lady Acton; are you all right?" Mary asked in a quiet aside, as they were ushered off the boat. "Do you need to lie down?"

"A touch of seasickness, is all," Doyle lied. "I'll be fine, once I'm safe on land again."

"Let me know," Mary advised, as she linked her arm through Doyle's in a show of support. "We can always head home."

"I'll be fine, Mary," Doyle assured her, as she mustered up a smile. "And besides, the children would mutiny if we tried to cut the outin' short."

"Very true," Mary laughed, but hard on her words there was suddenly a startled child's cry, followed by a loud splash.

"It's Miss Gemma—no worries, I've got her," Adrian announced, as he swiftly hoisted the little girl back up onto the dock by the back of her jacket.

"Oh, Gemma," Mary chided, as she enveloped her daughter in a hug. "Are you all right? You're the last one I'd expect to fall in."

But the girl eyed her male companions reproachfully. "Someone pushed me."

"Not me," Emile said immediately, and it was true.

"No matter," Doyle said quickly, hoping it wasn't Edward.

Mary rose and took the girl's hand. "We'll head home—she'll need to change out of her wet clothes."

Immediately, a howl of protest rose up from Emile and Doyle's boys, and amidst the din Adrian offered, "There's a blanket in the limo; I'll be happy to take her home to get her sorted, then bring her back."

"Oh—thank you, Mr. Adrian, I'm so sorry for the inconvenience."

"No problem," said Adrian, who didn't much want to hang around Callie and Seamus in the first place. "Come along, Miss Gemma—here's my jacket."

"Everyone stay close," Trenton advised rather sternly. "No pushing."

"I didn't push her," Edward protested, and Doyle duly noted that this was true, which left little Tommy as the culprit, although it was unlikely he'd done such a thing intentionally—hard to believe he was even strong enough to do the deed.

Taking the toddler's hand in an excess of caution, Doyle herded the group toward the building's entry-door, where Rolph appeared almost immediately as the glass doors slid open for them. "Come on in, how was the boat ride?" he asked, the question mainly directed toward Miss Senak.

"It was very good," she replied with her shy smile. "It is so beautiful on the water."

"Wait 'til you see the inside," he advised proudly. "It's a cracker."

"Is it open?" asked Callie doubtfully. "There's no one inside."

Mary explained, "Rolph has offered to give the children a tour of the new science discovery museum—it's almost ready to open."

They walked into the spacious lobby area, and then climbed the broad, open stairway to the second-floor mezzanine, where the museum was located. There was still some construction equipment lying about, and plastic tarps covering the sleek benches that lined the mezzanine floor, but all in all, the place did seem nearly ready to open. Doyle covertly scanned the area, looking for anything that might be of use in establishing a case, but didn't see much of interest; the spacious entry lobby was uncluttered, with no suspicious-looking containers or any other items that would give her an opening to ask Rolph some questions.

They came into the museum area—their footsteps echoing on the wooden floor— and Rolph, rather self-importantly, began to explain the first display that they came across. "This one's about power sources; here's the water display—look, I'll demonstrate."

The boys watched as the young man pushed a pumping device so that water traveled up into a storage tank, and then he pulled a chain that released the water so that it cascaded down over a water wheel, causing it to spin. The impressive result was a visible electrical charge, produced in a long tube.

"Oh," marveled Miss Senak. "Is it hot?"

"Not at all—can't have something dangerous on display for the kiddos. Here, I'll show you."

He then took her hand and placed it on the tube, holding it beneath his own as the electricity crackled and sparked.

Worse and worse, thought Doyle in dismay, as the young couple suddenly seemed tongue-tied. Faith, there's far too much electricity in the air, and Rolph's a bad bet for poor Miss Senak —as I know only too well. Not to mention that his erstwhile father is slated to go to prison soon, fingers crossed. Ah well; this burgeoning romance will be snuffed-out soon enough, and there's little to be done in the meanwhile.

After everyone took an enthusiastic turn—even Tommy, hoisted up by Trenton—Rolph moved the boys to the next station, which allowed them to inject hydrogen gas into a hydrogen fuel cell—the resulting burst of power causing a toy carousel to spin 'round.

As the children were plastered against the glass, fascinated, Doyle could suddenly hear rapid footsteps approaching, as the thoroughly alarmed Mr. Elliott advanced upon them. "Mr. Denisovich!"

"Yeah, Walter?" Rolph drawled.

Outraged, the man sputtered, "You cannot allow unauthorized persons to be on premises."

But Rolph only shrugged. "Relax, we'll just be a minute. I wanted to show them the power-source display."

Elliott was unable to resist nervously glancing at Doyle, as he persisted, "You must clear them out, immediately. It is unsafe."

"No worries; we'll be on our way in a minute."

With poor grace, the man turned to retreat, and Doyle decided that this interaction gave her an opening to do a bit of probing. Giving Rolph an arch look, she asked, "What's he so worried about? Everythin' looks safe enough."

Rolph rolled his eyes. "He's an impossible fussbudget, and I'll be happy to see the last of him. Instead of getting the permitting completed, he spends all his time fawning over his precious artwork, and trying to decide what should be on the walls."

Tamping down her leap of excitement, Doyle made an effort to keep her tone neutral. "What sort of artwork? I'd love to see it —I'm very interested in art."

With a calculating glance toward the stairway—where Elliott

was descending whilst he spoke in low, unhappy tones on his mobile—Rolph replied, "Sure—come this way into the lounge area." He then explained to Miss Senak, "We're going to have a lounge area for the parents, right next to the museum. We'll advertise the shops and the restaurant, so that they'll want to go spend their money."

"That is very clever," Miss Senak exclaimed in admiration.

"I can't take credit," Rolph admitted. "But the people who made the floorplan definitely know their stuff."

"Let's go see that artwork," Doyle urged, as the boys began to chase one another around the exhibit. "The natives are gettin' restless."

CHAPTER 36

Rolph escorted the party into the lounge area, which seemed similar to a museum's gallery room—benches lined up in the middle of the room for seating, with the walls slated to display advertisements and art even though nothing had been hung, as yet. The benches were still covered with plastic, and an assortment of what looked to be large posters were leaning against one of the walls.

I should take a snap of this, Doyle decided quickly, and I should do it before our friend Mr. Elliott realizes that we're mucking about.

To this end, she asked Rolph, "Is the artwork for sale?"

"Now, that's a good idea," said Rolph, much struck. "Another moneymaker; I'm surprised my uncle hasn't thought of it yet."

"It *is* surprisin'," Doyle said innocently. "May I look?"

"I don't see the harm; if you like to buy something, just let me know and I'm sure I can arrange for it."

With no further ado, Doyle walked over, pulling her mobile to take some snaps of the large, colorful posters that were leaning in a stack against the wall.

The rest of the group wandered over to watch her, and so Doyle said brightly, "These are perfect—I'll just show Acton." Immediately, she suited word to deed and sent him a text.

"I don't think they're to his taste," Callie remarked doubtfully.

"He'll buy them for her," Rolph informed her with a touch of derision. "According to my uncle, Acton thinks the sun rises and sets on her."

"Oh—that is so sweet," said Miss Senak, oblivious to the young man's cynicism.

"I suppose," Rolph admitted, in a quick turnabout. "I suppose if you've got the money, you may as well spend it on your wife."

But Riordan was frowning, as he bent to scrutinize the outermost poster in the stack. "Hold a moment; this one was in the storage room at the library where I worked. It's a Chéret—I recognize it."

Callie said a bit skeptically, "Unlikely it's the same one, Seamus. I imagine there are quite a few copies—everyone loves these art-deco posters."

"*Fin de siècle*," Riordan corrected absently, his brow knit. "I'm certain it's the same one. See the mark, just here? That's where the library's inventory tag was."

"A small world," Doyle pronounced in a jovial tone, as she took his arm and firmly steered him away. Under her breath, she advised the young man in Gaelic, "Hush; keep walkin'."

"Right," he agreed, startled.

With a casual air, she took up her mobile and texted Acton. "S saw goods can ID."

"Good; on my way," came the immediate response. "Get clear."

Placing a hand on Edward's forehead, Doyle made a show of motherly concern. Faith, I'm wonderin' if you're a bit feverish."

"Mum," the boy protested, squirming away. "I'm fine."

"Time to head home, I think."

As could be expected, this announcement was met with a chorus of objections but Doyle held firm, and after sizing up the exits with a copper's eye, she suggested that they walk through the lounge so as to head down the back-exit stairway. "It's closer to the parkin' lot," she explained, when her actual intent was to keep them well-away from the building's street entry, where Acton and his officers would be soon be making an appearance. They should be well-clear when the coppers showed up—and wasn't it a stroke of good luck, that Riordan happened to be here to identify an artwork he'd seen in Dublin. Faith, this whole recon operation couldn't have worked out better, and apparently the ghost—despite Doyle's many doubts—had been steering her aright, all along.

She paused for a moment, thinking. It would probably behoove her to send Riordan in Acton's direction, in the event Elliott tried to bar the door and demand a warrant whilst he destroyed any evidence of wrongdoing. If Seamus was at hand, Acton could then use the young man's testimony on the spot so as to force his way in.

"Take Mr. Riordan around toward the front entry, on the street-side," she instructed Trenton. "Acton's goin' in with a team

—let him know you'll be hangin' about if Mr. Riordan is needed. But don't let anyone see him without Acton's say-so, and don't leave him by himself."

"Yes, ma'am," Trenton nodded.

To Riordan, Doyle instructed, "You'll go with Trenton, Mr. Riordan."

"What?" asked Callie in surprise. "What about me?"

"You'll go home, Callie," Doyle replied. "I'll explain later."

"But I don't want to go home," Callie complained, clearly unhappy with this turn of events.

"Hush," Doyle cautioned. "This is police business—go home."

"Oh," the girl said, her eyes wide. "Sorry."

"No worries—you can walk out with them." This would be helpful, in that—if anyone was watching them, thanks to Elliott's warning—it wouldn't raise suspicion to see a young couple exit the place, rather than Riordan with Trenton. "But don't dilly-dally." She gave Trenton a meaningful look, and he nodded; best get them clear before the cavalry charged in.

CHAPTER 37

As Doyle turned to gather-up the rest of her party, Rolph said to Miss Senak, "A shame you have to cut it short. I could give you a tour of the restaurant, if you'd like to stay."

"Everyone's leaving," Doyle said firmly, even though she couldn't truly control what Miss Senak would do. "Let's all thank Mr. Denisovich."

As the children dutifully delivered their thanks, Mary pulled her phone, "Let me text Mr. Adrian and tell him we're headed back."

"Oh—good thought," said Doyle, since the last needful thing was to have Gemma wandering about whilst a potential take-down was unfolding. "But let's all keep movin'—this way, everybody."

After her text, Mary addressed Miss Senak. "If you like to come home with us, I can show you around."

With a beaming smile of gratitude, Miss Senak replied, "Oh—oh, yes; oh, thank you, Mrs. Savoie."

"Perfect," Doyle said, as she gestured them along. "Off we go."

"You'll need a key to open the exit," Rolph explained as he self-importantly produced a ring of keys. "Until we have the permits, everything's locked down."

After he'd unlocked the door, Rolph continued to hover in an annoying fashion and so Doyle firmly bade him goodbye—yet again—before herding everyone through and shutting the door behind them with a clang. Safe and sound, she thought with some relief; and with the evidence all tied up in a neat little bow. Well-done, Officer Doyle—and a surprising well-done to the late Sasha Lanska, too.

The children began noisily descending the stairs—calling out, to hear their voices echo off the walls—with Tommy steadfastedly rejecting Doyle's hand because the other boys weren't holding anyone's hand. As a result, progress was necessarily a bit slow as the three young women made their way down the two flights of stairs. The stairwell itself appeared to be unfinished, since the walls weren't painted and the suspended ceiling hadn't yet been laid-in; they could see the exposed wire t-bars and ducting above their heads.

As they patiently waited for Tommy to navigate each stair, Mary took the opportunity to ask Doyle in a quiet aside, "How are you feeling?"

"All's well," Doyle replied cheerfully, since it was true.

"Miss Senak is perfect," Mary assured her, mainly because

Mary was the next thing to a saint, and thought everyone was perfect.

Doyle made a wry mouth. "Well, here's hopin' Rolph doesn't come 'round, tryin' to cast his lures—can't imagine Savoie would tolerate such a thing."

"It was rather sweet," Mary pronounced, an indulgent smile directed at Miss Senak's back. "You wouldn't think Miss Senak would be his type."

"I wouldn't think anyone was," Doyle answered in a tart tone, and Mary laughed.

They came to the ground floor, where Emile was pushing on the exit bar, thoroughly frustrated. "It's stuck," the boy complained.

"Let me try," said Mary, who gave it a hard push, but still the door did not budge.

"It feels like the push-bar isn't attached to the locking mechanism," Doyle decided, as she gave it a turn.

"Well, that's a bother—it must need a key from the outside. Let's go up, again," Mary announced to the children. "We'll have a race."

There was a wild rush up the stairway, and whilst the three young women followed them at a more leisurely pace. Mary offered, "They probably haven't had a final inspection yet—you can see that it isn't yet finished."

"Or the door's been disabled, because they don't want anyone to have access 'til the building's ready," Doyle pointed out, which seemed more likely, considering the place's questionable goings-on.

"Our bad luck," said Mary cheerfully to Miss Senak. "It's good exercise, I suppose."

But Doyle was suddenly finding that their return trek up the stairwell—as their footsteps echoed off the narrow walls—invoked an eerie sense of deja-view, or whatever it was called. She'd been trapped in a stairwell once before—speaking of Philippe Savoie—and the unbidden memory was making her very uneasy. Therefore, she was almost unsurprised when she heard Emile exclaim that the door to the lounge wasn't opening, either.

"How can that be?" asked Mary in surprise. "We just came through."

"It may be the same case as the lower door," Doyle guessed. "It's been disabled to keep people out. Let me call for help."

She attempted to ring-up Adrian, but was immediately met with a "no service" icon. "Faith; we're well-and-truly stuck," she joked to Mary and Miss Senak. "I suppose we could try to shout for help, but it's unlikely there's anyone about who can hear us."

"I'm hungry," Emile complained, in the time-honored manner of boys who were growing like a weed.

Mary teased, "I hope you don't starve to death before we're rescued."

"Not to worry," Doyle assured the boy. "Mr. Trenton or Lord Acton will figure out that we're stuck in here—we should have a wager about how long it will be before we're freed."

This idea was met with a great deal of enthusiasm, as everyone chose a set number of minutes—even Tommy who thought that "one" was a good bet.

And mayhap it is, thought Doyle; any minute now there should be plenty of people crawling about, one of them being my wedded husband who is probably wondering at this very moment why his wife has not cleared-out as she's been asked. All will be well; if only—if only this situation wasn't giving me flashbacks to the Wexton Prison stairwell, even though that comparison seems absurd. We may have been inconvenienced, but we're in no danger, surely, and Acton will come to let us out in short order—I need only be patient. It's a shame that I'm distracting the man from his important take-down, but who could have known that the stupid stairwell would present such a hazard, and I'd have no one at hand to help?

Doyle's scalp prickled, and she suddenly realized that she was without either one of her security-men—a very unusual occurrence. Of course, it couldn't be helped, the way events had unfolded, but nevertheless it only compounded her feeling that something wasn't right. Both security-men were absent, her phone wasn't working, and Acton didn't know where she was. Faith, what were the odds?

A bit hesitantly, Mary ventured, "Do you smell smoke, or is it just me?"

With some alarm, Doyle glanced above them and saw that a light haze was visible in the industrial crawlspace overhead. Something was burning—there was a fire, somewhere, and the fire-proof stairwell could prove to be a death-trap, since the ceiling wasn't yet sealed but the doors were; even as she watched, the smoky haze was getting thicker overhead, and soon it would be difficult to breathe.

"We've got to get out," she announced briskly. "I'll need you two to hoist me up into the crawlspace, and I'll go for help."

"All right," Mary agreed, her lips pale even though her expression was composed. "Should we hoist Emile, instead? We can easily lift him between us, and he'll do what he's told."

"Right," Doyle agreed, since this did seem a better plan—Emile was lighter and a much better wriggler than Doyle. She leaned against the wall and cupped her hands for his foot. "Up you go, Emile; find a way out—kick out a vent, if you have to—and then run as fast as you can toward the front of the building, the entry on the street—there should be plenty of people about. Pull any fire alarms you see on the way, but they may not be workin'. The most important thing is to get to the entry doors as fast as you can."

"Yes, ma'am," said Emile, as he clambered up to stand on Doyle's shoulders, his hands bracing against the wall.

"Can I go, too?" asked Edward.

"You'll stay right here," his mother advised, as Mary—who was taller than Doyle—had Emile step onto her raised hands so as to give him an added boost.

His hand clutching at the sidewall's edge, Emile scrambled into the crawlspace area, catching hold of the wire suspensions and quickly navigating his way out of sight.

"He was always the king of the monkey-bars," Doyle remarked, and Mary managed to muster up a small, nervous smile.

CHAPTER 38

They all settled-in to sit on the stairs, the three women anxiously watching the door as though willing it to open, whilst the haze of smoke grew thicker and thicker.

Acton knows we're not clear, Doyle assured herself; and he'll scrub his take-down in a second, if he has to. It's maddening, that we're trapped in here with the place on fire—such a crackin' crazy turn of events. But I'd a feeling—I'd a feeling, I did, and it's a shame that the feeling came far too late to do anything about it.

No, her instinct told her. The dog was a portent.

Thoroughly confused, Doyle frowned as she kept her gaze fixed on the door. Seamus Riordan had seen a dog—Raven, perhaps? But the fair Doyle hadn't seen him, which was a bit strange, come to think of it, and meant that mayhap it wasn't Raven a'tall, since poor Gemma had wound-up in the drink and you'd think Raven would have prevented such a thing—

Her scalp prickled, and suddenly she stilled. Holy *Mother*, she realized with dawning horror; Holy Mother of God—it *was* Raven, and he'd pushed Gemma into the water. Pushed her in, because none of this is a coincidence, and I've been led here like a mouse into a trap—led into a trap with Savoie's family right beside me.

She closed her eyes briefly, trying to convince herself that such was not the case even though she knew—in the way that she knew things—that the ghost of Sasha Lanska was behind this bizarre chain of events. *The wheel is come full circle*, she'd said, and Savoie's family was going to be burnt to death—the same vengeance that Savoie had meted out to Lanska, herself. She wanted to make things right, she kept saying, and Doyle—like a fool—didn't consider that "right" to someone like her would mean bloodthirsty vengeance.

It's like her favorite play—she's bent on slaughtering her enemy's family, Doyle realized with a sickening sense of bleak dismay; and she's managed to accomplish it with the fey Doyle serving as the handy means to an end. What better way to get her own back at Savoie than to destroy his family—it would devastate him, not to mention that Gemma's death would serve as the icing on the evil cake. Mother a' Mercy, but Doyle was a fool to have taken the woman's advice—a fool not to have recognized what was afoot, when Riordan had told her that Raven had shown-up—shown-up and neatly removed Gemma from all danger.

Her horrified thoughts were interrupted when little Tommy started coughing. "Perhaps we should head downstairs again—the air will be fresher," Mary ventured, and Doyle could hear the suppressed fear in her voice. It was a race against the clock, and it was not a'tall clear that Emile would get them help in time—not to mention that they were behind a fire-door, so that even if Acton knew they were in here, it would take a massive effort to break them out.

"Aye, let's go," Doyle agreed, trying to keep her voice even. As she gathered Tommy up, the little boy began crying into her shoulder because he didn't understand what was happening, save that his mother was frightened and his mother didn't scare easy.

Taking firm hold of herself, Doyle ducked her head and said to the little boy in a steady tone, "Hush, Tommy; Emile's getting help and he's a clever boy—any minute now." And surely Acton was on his way—he was a more than a match for any paltry ghost, no matter how steeped in evil.

"Let's sing a hymn," Mary suggested. "Who wants to choose?"

Edward piped up, "I like the one that goes, 'Give me oil in my lamp, keep me burning, burning, burning'."

"Perfect," said Mary with a straight face. "Now, everyone scoot on your bums down the stairs—follow Miss Senak."

But just as they began this process, the lounge door sprang open, and a rush of fresh air came in with it. Doyle thought she'd never be so happy to behold Rolph, holding a handkerchief over his nose and mouth and with Emile crouching behind him.

Rolph shouted, "Quickly, there's a fire—you all need to get downstairs, now!"

Holy Mother, I can't let the door close, Doyle thought frantically, and lunged toward it only to find that Emile had held the same thought, and wedged himself against the jamb behind Rolph.

"No, no," said Rolph, tugging at Emile. "Let it close; we have to keep the smoke out."

"The door's locked below—I think it needs to be unlocked from the outside," Doyle explained in a rush. "This is the only way out."

Rolph stared at her for a moment, and his gaze traveled to Miss Senak, who was openly weeping into her palms. "Right—let's go out this way, then. Stay low, and follow me—I know the schematics, and there's a maintenance hallway door just down the wall. It will lead us to the access on the balcony, and once we're there, we can be seen."

"Right," Doyle agreed in relief. "Quickly, now—everyone hold hands and follow Rolph."

"I'll take him," Rolph offered, reaching for Tommy as Doyle filed past.

"I don't think I can leave him go," Doyle admitted. "Take Hannah, instead."

In short order, they were scurrying low along the wall in the lounge area, the smoke so thick that it was getting hard to see, and Doyle struggling to carry Tommy. They came to the maintenance door, and Rolph tried a few different keys before it blessedly clicked, and then they all hurried through, with Rolph slamming the door shut behind them.

"Well done, Rolph and Emile," Mary said, as they all paused in relief.

"Yes, yes, thank you—thank you," Miss Senak wept. "I was so frightened."

"You're safe, I'll get you out," Rolph assured her as he took her hand.

Doyle, who'd no time for this, urged, "Let's go—we're not out of the woods yet." This was evident; the air was a bit clearer in the dim hallway, but the smoky haze was nonetheless descending overhead.

"This way," Rolph directed.

"I hear sirens," said Emile.

"Thank God fastin'," Doyle exclaimed in massive relief. "Stay right behind me, Edward, and don't stray."

Clutching Tommy, she followed close behind Rolph and Miss Senak—Rolph still carrying Hannah—as Edward, Mary and Emile brought up the rear.

"Damn, but this was the worst luck in the world," Rolph complained.

"D'you know what happened?" asked Doyle, who was keenly aware that luck had nothing to do with it.

The young man offered over his shoulder, "I'm not sure, actually. I went up to the roof-terrace—watching for your party to come out through the parking lot, but you never did. I came down to investigate, and saw the fire—it looked like that pile of posters had caught fire. Then the boy kicked out a vent, and so I helped him down."

Doyle nodded, and surmised that Mr. Elliott must have panicked when he caught wind that the coppers were coming, and—in the manner of dim-witted bureaucrats everywhere—he made a bad situation worse by trying to destroy the evidence. Thank all the blessed saints and holy angels that Rolph was love-struck, and trying to catch one last glimpse of Miss Senak.

Hard on this thought, Rolph assured Miss Senak, "We'll get to the balcony and wait for rescue. Don't be afraid."

But almost before the words echoed away, there was a huge blast that made the very walls rattle, and they all cried out as they steadied themselves.

"Holy smoke," Rolph exclaimed. "What's that?"

"It sounded like a bomb," Emile ventured.

"It's coming from up ahead." Rolph hesitated. "Maybe we should retreat back the other way."

"I think it might be the hydrogen," said Doyle, dredging up her hazardous materials training. Hydrogen is flammable."

As soon as she said the words, another explosion shook the walls, and the smaller children—thoroughly startled—began to cry.

"Not good," said Rolph. "There's a bunch of hydrogen cannisters stockpiled for the power-source exhibit, but we need to get to the balcony. I think we have to keep going—we can always jump into the water."

Mother a' Mercy, it wants only this, thought Doyle.

Running as fast as they were able, another explosion rocked them just as they came to the end of the hallway, where Rolph flung open the access door so that they emerged onto the broad balcony.

"Keep goin', don't look back," Doyle shouted to Edward, but she was unable to resist a glance behind her, and saw that the entire museum room was engulfed in fire. As she watched, another explosion caused an extra flare of flames to leap from the inferno, shaking the floor of the balcony.

"Let's get into the water—quick, quick, quick," shouted Rolph. "The balcony's catching fire."

But the sirens were blaring and Doyle hesitated; the surface of the water seemed a long way down, and surely, surely rescue was at hand? "Tommy can't swim," she shouted. No need to mention that neither could she.

"We can't wait," Rolph shouted back. "It's all right; I'll go first, and then I'll catch the little kids."

"Me, too," Emile declared, as he immediately scrambled atop the railing, and then leapt out over the dock-way below without a moment's hesitation.

He landed in the water with a huge splash, and then turned to shout, "Throw Hannah—I'll catch her."

"Oh—" Mary protested in dismay.

"Let me go first, and I'll help him catch her," Rolph directed, as he handed the toddler to Mary.

But as Rolph gripped the railing to leap over, Miss Senak tearfully beseeched; "No—don't leave me; I—I cannot do this, I cannot jump."

"Come with me, then," Rolph instructed, as he grabbed at her necklace. "Wind the pearls around your wrist; I'll hold the other end, and we'll go together—Bob's your uncle."

Rather forcefully, he hauled the young woman after him up the railing. "Here we go." The couple then leapt out, and plunged into the water—landing beside Emile, who seemed to be rather enjoying himself.

Another explosion shook the balcony, and Doyle only managed to keep her feet by freeing a hand to clutch at the rail. With Tommy wailing in her ear, she frantically looked for

Edward only to see that the boy was already leaping though the air, intent on joining Emile.

Her heart hammering in her breast, she watched as her son's head emerged from the water beside Rolph, who then buoyed him up and pushed him over to the dock's edge.

"C'mon, Hannah," Emile called out. "Toss her, mum."

Nothin' for it, Doyle thought with grim determination. With the flames roaring behind them, she shouted to Mary, "I'll toss yours, and you'll toss mine. On three; one, two—"

"—blessed art thou amongst women—" Mary murmured under her breath, as she forcibly pulled Tommy from Doyle, and turned to throw him.

"Three!" Her arms already exhausted from carrying Tommy, Doyle mustered all of her strength and tossed the wailing Hannah into the air, but even as she did, she was suddenly lifted off her feet by a huge explosion behind her. The balcony seemed to give way beneath her and she felt herself falling—suspended in the air with the water's surface fast-approaching, her stomach knotted in a feeling that was as familiar as it was unwelcome.

CHAPTER 39

He couldn't think about her ordeal without becoming enraged, so instead he focused on what needed to be done.

Doyle found it rather pleasant, to be drifting about in this nothingness that was nevertheless so vivid and intense—rather like one of her dreams, save without the pesky ghosts who were always demanding her attention. Truly a relief of sorts, to be able to feel without thinking, for a change.

Enough of this, she told herself firmly; you're needed.

After an unsuccessful attempt or two, she managed to open her eyes and found that she was staring at the embroidered canopy that stretched over the master's bed at Trestles. She gazed at it for a moment, admiring the needlework and trying to pull her wits together.

"Kathleen?"

"Yes," she whispered, and turned to look for him—no real

need, because he'd leapt up and was now hovering over her, scrutinizing her face.

Oh-oh, she thought, and managed to muster-up a small smile of reassurance. "Hallo, Michael."

In a show of relief—unusual for him—he closed his eyes briefly.

"What's happened?" Suddenly, the memory came rushing back and she clutched at his arm in alarm. "The boyos?"

"Everyone is fine," he assured her. "They're downstairs."

Since he didn't volunteer anything further, she decided she may as well ask again, "What's happened?"

"You were deprived of oxygen for a short time, and so the hospital instituted a coma protocol to curtail the swelling in your brain. "Let me fetch Tim to examine you—he's here."

But she kept her hand on his arm so as to stay him. "I'm sorry I gave you such a scare, Michael. All's well, my promise."

He nodded, but made no response.

So; all's not well, she concluded. I wonder how scorched the earth is.

"The baby's fine," she advised.

"Yes. They checked her heartbeat at the hospital."

She smiled slightly. "She's too little to be bothered."

"Indeed."

Doyle took-in her husband's drawn face, and contemplated the interesting fact that he seemed reluctant to tell her how she'd managed to land here in the master's suite at Trestles. Along those lines, she decided it was pertinent to point out, "You've a shiner."

"Yes," he agreed, and offered nothing further.

Gently, she teased, "Hard to believe anyone got close enough to black your eye, Michael."

He did not respond—he was struggling, poor man—and so she changed the subject. "Did anyone else get hurt? Mary?"

"Bumps and bruises—both Mary and Tommy. No one was severely injured."

She smiled in relief. "Thank God fastin'. And thanks to—of all people—Rolph, who turned-up a champ."

He bent his head in acknowledgment at her wondering tone. "Yes. I've read the report."

This was of interest, in that it implied that he hadn't been involved in the making of the report. "Who would have thought that our Rolph would turn out to be a Jonathan?"

He lifted his gaze to meet hers again, silent for a moment. "I am afraid I don't follow."

"Jonathan was David's best friend, but Jonathan's father was King Saul. When he had to choose between them, he betrayed his father to help David."

Acton tilted his head. "I'm not certain that Rolph was aware he was betraying his father."

"Now, there's a good point. "So—he's not the Jonathan, after all. More like the romantic hero in one of those novels, right down to the tremblin' maiden in distress."

There was a small silence whilst they regarded each other. Her husband was shuttered-in, and it was hard to read what he was thinking behind his darker-than-usual eyes. He didn't do well when she was put at-risk, and this one was probably the topper—he was in a black mood like no other, and he was being very, very careful with his words. She'd not press him, though; there would be time enough, and she'd the feeling that this was going to take some careful handling.

Hoping to remind him of silver linings, she asked, "Did you manage to roll-up Denisovich?"

"The take-down was necessarily abandoned, because Mr. Riordan came forward to alert me to your circumstance."

Doyle waded through this aristo-speak with some misgiving. "Oh. Well, good on him."

"Yes. You'd sunk beneath the surface, but he knew exactly where you were."

There was a small silence. "That's lucky," she ventured, but he made no reply.

Oh-oh, she thought, and decided to change the subject yet again. "A shame, that after all this trouble your wretched take-down will have to wait for another day."

"No longer necessary; Igor Denisovich is dead." This news delivered in an even tone and without a flicker of emotion.

She lifted her brows. "Is that so?"

"It is."

She was to be given no further insights, and—on the tiny chance that he didn't know where the blame should squarely fall—she informed him, "Mr. Elliott's the one who started the fire—he was tryin' to destroy the evidence."

"Yes, I am aware."

"Well, I hope he's been rolled-up, at least."

"Mr. Elliott is also dead," her husband advised.

She eyed him for a moment. "Anyone else?"

He didn't answer the question, but rose to kiss her forehead.

"Let me fetch Tim; he wanted to check your brain functions as soon as you woke."

"He may have to search long and hard," she teased.

But her husband didn't seem to find this sally amusing, and said only, "I will be right back—will you be all right?"

This was of interest, in that it seemed there wasn't anyone else at hand—the place did seem strangely quiet. And since Doyle well-knew the antidote for quietness, she advised, "Send the boys up along with Tim, please."

He hesitated at the door. "Perhaps after your examination."

"Perhaps now," she countered firmly. "Along with a sandwich—I'm starvin'."

He bowed his head. "Very well."

He carefully shut the door behind him, and as her thoughtful gaze rested upon it, she said into the silence, "Mad as a March hare."

Made in the USA
Middletown, DE
13 March 2024

51376738R00146